VAMPIRE
HUNTER D

Other Vampire Hunter D books published by
Dark Horse Books and Digital Manga Publishing

VAMPIRE HUNTER D

VOLUME 3
DEMON DEATHCHASE

Written by
HIDEYUKI KIKUCHI

Illustrations by
YOSHITAKA AMANO

English translation by
KEVIN LEAHY

Dark Horse Books®
Milwaukie

Los Angeles

VAMPIRE HUNTER D 3: DEMON DEATHCHASE

Cover art by Yoshitaka Amano.

English translation by Kevin Leahy

Book Design by Heidi Fainza

Published by
Dark Horse Books
a division of Dark Horse Comics
10956 SE Main Street
Milwaukie, OR 97222
darkhorse.com

Digital Manga Publishing
1487 West 178th Street, Suite 300
Gardena, CA 90248
dmpbooks.com

Library of Congress Cataloging-in-Publication Data is available upon request.

ISBN-10: 1-59582-031-0
ISBN-13: 978-1-59582-031-0

First printing: January 2006

10 9 8 7 6 5 4 3 2

Printed in the United States of America

VAMPIRE HUNTER D

I

T he tiny village obstinately refused the blessings the sunlight poured down so generously upon it.

Though a Frontier village like this might see its share of years, as a rule the size of the community didn't fluctuate greatly. The village's eighty or so homes wavered in the warming light. Every last bit of the lingering snow had been consumed by the black soil. Spring was near.

And yet, the village was dead.

Doors of reinforced plastic and treated lumber hung open, swinging with the feeble breeze. In the communal cookery, which should have been roiling with the lively voices of wives and children as evening approached, now dust danced alone.

Something was missing. People.

The majority of the homes remained in perfect order, with no signs of any struggle by the occupants, but in one or two there were overturned chairs in the living room. In one house, the bed covers were disheveled, as if someone just settling down to sleep had gotten out of bed to attend to some trifling matter.

Had gotten out—and had never come back.

Small black stains could be found on the floors of that house. A number of spots no bigger than the tip of your little finger, they might be mistaken for a bit of fur off a pet dog or cat. The spots wouldn't catch anyone's eye. Even if they would, there were no people around with eyes to be caught.

Evening grew near, the white sunlight took on a dim bluish tint, the wind blowing down the deserted streets grew more insistent, and an eerie atmosphere pervaded the village at dusk—like ebon silhouettes were coalescing in the shadows and training their bloodshot gaze on any travelers that might pass through the wide-open gates.

More time passed. Just when the dim shadows were beginning to linger in the streets, the sound of iron-shod hooves pounding the earth, and the crunch of tires in well-worn ruts, came drifting in through the entrance to the village.

A bus and three people on horseback came to a halt in front of one of the watch towers just inside the gates.

The atomic-powered bus was the sort used for communications across the Frontier, but its body had been modified, so that now iron bars were set into the windows and a trenchant plow was affixed to the front of the vehicle. Not exactly the sort of vehicle upstanding folks had much call for.

Every inch of the vehicle was jet black—a perfect complement to the foreboding air of the trio looming before it.

"What the hell's going on here?" asked the man on the right. He wore a black shirt and black leather pants. Conspicuous for his fierce expression and frightfully long torso, this man would stand out anywhere.

"Don't look like our client's here to meet us," said the man on the far left. Though his face wore a wry smile, his thread-thin eyes brimmed with a terrible light as they scoured his surroundings. A hexagonal staff strapped to his well-defined back made his shadow appear impaled.

As if on cue, the two turned their heads toward the even more muscular giant standing between them. From neck to wrist, his body was covered by a protector of thin metal on leather, but the mountain of muscles beneath it was still sharply defined. His face was like a chunk of granite that had sprouted whiskers, and he brimmed with an intensity that would make a bear backpedal if it ran across him in the dark. Twining around him, the wind seemed to carry the stench of a beast as it blew off again.

"Looks like they've had it," he muttered in a stony tone. "The whole damn village gone in one night—looks like we lost the goose that laid the golden egg. Just to be sure, let's check out a few houses. Carefully."

"I ain't too crazy about that idea," the man in black said. "How 'bout we send Grove? For him it'd—" His voice died out halfway through the sentence. The giant had shot a glance at him. It was like being scrutinized by a stone. "I . . . er . . . I was just kidding, bro."

It wasn't merely the difference in their builds that made the man in black grow pale—it appeared that the man truly feared the giant. Quickly dismounting—the man with the hexagonal staff did likewise—they then entered the village with a gliding gait.

There was the sound of the bus door opening. The face of a girl with blonde hair peered out at the giant from the driver's seat. "Borgoff, what's up?" she asked. At twenty-two or -three years old, her visage was as lovely as a blossom, but there was something about how overly alluring it was that called to mind a carnivorous insect—beautiful but deadly.

"Odds are the village's been wasted. Be ready to move on a moment's notice." Saying that in a subdued tone, the world seemed to go topsy-turvy as his voice suddenly became gentle. "How's Grove?" he inquired.

"He's okay for the moment. Not likely to have another seizure for a while."

It was unclear whether or not the giant heard the girl's response, as he didn't so much as nod but kept gazing at the silent, lonely rows of houses. He flicked his eyes up toward the sky and the dingy, ivory hue that lingered there. The round moon was already showing its pearly white figure.

"Wish we had a little more cloud cover."

Just as he'd muttered those words, two figures came speeding down the street as if riding the very wind.

"It's just like we thought. Not a single freaking person," the man in black said.

The man with the hexagonal staff turned to the sky and said, "Sun'll be setting soon. The safest bet would be to blow this place as soon as possible, big guy." Saying that, he jabbed out his forefinger.

Apparently, the giant easily pierced the hazy darkness to glimpse the tiny black spot on the tip of that finger.

"Make for the graveyard," he said.

In a flash, a tense hue shot through the faces of the other men, but soon enough they, too, grinned, climbed effortlessly back on their horses, and boldly started their mounts down village streets that'd fallen into the stillness of death.

†

So what had transpired in the village?

Having the entire populace of a place disappear in one fell swoop wasn't such a bizarre occurrence on the Frontier. For example, the carnivorous balloon-like creatures known as flying jellyfish seemed to produce an extremely large specimen at a rate of one every twenty years or so. The beast was often a mile and a quarter in diameter, and it could cover an entire village, selectively dissolving every living creature before sucking them all up into its maw.

And then there was the basilisk. A magical creature said to inhabit only deep mountain ravines and haunted valleys, it had merely to wait at the entrance to a village and stare fixedly at a given spot within. Its single, gigantic eye would glow a reddish tint before finally releasing a crimson beam, and villagers would come, first one, then another, right into its fearsome waiting jaws. But the sole weakness of the basilisk was that occasionally one of the hypnotized humans would bid farewell to their family, and when they did so it was always in exactly the same words. Hearing those words, the remaining folk would go out and hunt the basilisk en masse.

However, the most likely cause of every last person vanishing from an entire village was both the most familiar of threats and the most terrifying.

When news of such an eerie happening was passed along by even a single traveler lucky enough to have slipped through such a community unharmed, people could practically hear the footfalls of their dark lords, supposedly long since extinct, lingering in that area. The masters of the darkness—the vampires.

†

H aving arrived at the graveyard on the edge of town, the trio of riders and the lone vehicle came to an abrupt halt. In a spot not five hundred yards from the forest, moss-encrusted gravestones formed serpentine rows, and there was an open space where, little by little, the blue-black darkness rose from the ground.

The fearsome trio strode forward, keeping their eyes on everything, coming to a halt in the depths of a forest that threatened to overrun the tombstones. From that spot alone, an area where something had turned over a large expanse of ground to reveal the red clay and left it looking like a subterranean demon had run amuck, there blew a weird miasma. It was a presence so ghastly it froze the leading pair atop their horses and made the giant swallow so hard his Adam's apple thumped in his throat.

What lay concealed by this ravaged earth?

Moving only their eyes, the men scanned the area in search of the source of the miasma.

It was then that they heard a dull sound.

No, it wasn't a sound, but rather a voice. A long, low groan—tormented and unabashed, like a patient having a seizure—began to snake through the uncanny tableau.

The men didn't move.

Partly it was the ghastly miasma, twisting tight around their bones, that prevented them from moving. But more than anything, they were still because that voice, those moans, seemed to issue from within the bus. When the giant had asked, hadn't the girl said he wouldn't have a seizure? It must've been the bizarre atmosphere billowing through this place that made a liar of her. Or perhaps his cries were because, no matter what illness afflicted them, there was something humans found horribly unsettling and inescapable about their mortal condition.

A few seconds later, a figure appeared from behind one of the massive tree trunks, as if to offer some answer to the riddle.

A veritable ghost, it stepped its way across the red clay in a precarious gait, coming to a standstill at a spot about thirty feet ahead of them.

The figure that loomed before the glimmering silver moon was that of an older man of fifty or so. With a dignified countenance and silver hair that seemed to give off a whitish glow of its own, anyone would've taken him for a village elder. Actually, however, this old man was doing two things that, when witnessed by those who knew about such matters, were as disturbing as anything could possibly be.

He was using his left hand to pin his jacket, with its upturned collar, to his chest, while his open right hand covered his mouth. As if to conceal his teeth.

"Thank you for coming," the old man said. His voice seemed pained, like something he'd just managed to vomit up. "Thank you for coming . . . but you're too late . . . Every last soul in the village *is done for*, myself included, but . . . "

Surely the fearsome men must've noticed that, as he spoke, the old man didn't turn his eyes on them.

There was nothing before his pupils, stagnant and muddied like those of a dead fish. Only a long line of trees continuing on into the abruptly growing darkness.

"Hurry, go after him. He—he made off with my daughter. Please, hurry after them and get her back . . . Or if she's already one of them . . . please make her end a quick one . . . "

Appealing, entreating, the old man went on in his reed-thin voice. Not so much as glancing at the men before him, he faced an empty spot between the trees. With the darkness so dear to demons steadily creeping in around them, it was an unsettling sight.

"He'd been after my daughter for a while. Time after time he tried to take her, and each and every time I fought him off. But last night, he finally showed his fangs . . . Once he got one of us, the rest fell like dominoes . . . I'm begging you, save my daughter from that accursed fate. Last night, he . . . took off to the north. With your speed, there might still be time . . . If you manage to save my daughter, go to the town of Galiusha. My younger sister's there. If you explain the situation, she'll give you the ten million dalas I promised . . . I beg of you . . . "

At this point in the old man's speech, the heap of dirt behind him underwent a change.

A small mound bulged up suddenly, and then a pale hand burst through the dirt. Resembling the dead man's hand flowers that bloomed only by night, this was in fact a real hand.

A deep grumbling filled the forest. Sheer malice, or a curse, the grumbling bore a thirst. An unquenchable thirst for blood, lasting for all eternity.

The figures pushing through the dirt and rising one after another were the villagers, transformed into vampires in the span of a single night.

Appearing just as they had in life, only now with complexions as sickly pale as paraffin, when the moonlight struck them they glowed with an eerie, pale, blue light.

There were burly men. There were dainty women. There were girls in dresses. There were boys in short pants. Nearly five hundred strong, their bloodshot eyes gleaming and their mouths set, words like unearthly or ghastly couldn't capture the way they stared intently at the men. They didn't even bother to knock off the dirt that clung to their heads and shoulders.

"Oh, it's too late now. Kill us somehow and get out of here . . . Once it's really night . . . I'll be . . . " The old man's left hand dropped. The pair of wounds that remained on the nape of his neck also showed on those of the other villagers.

It's hard to say which happened first—the old man lowering his right hand, or the men's jaws dropping. For between his lips thrown perilously wide, a pair of fangs jutted from the upper gums.

"Yeah, now it's getting interesting," the man in black said in an understandably tense tone, reaching for the crescent blades at his waist.

Perhaps the eldritch spell that held them had been broken, for the hands of the man with the hexagonal staff were gliding to his weapon.

The old man zipped effortlessly forward. Along with the mob at his back.

"Giddyup!" As if this was just what he'd been waiting for, the man in black spurred his horse into action. The man with the hexagonal staff followed after him, but the giant waited behind.

A number of the villagers had their heads staved in under the hooves, falling backward only to have their sternums and abdomens trampled as well.

"What are you waiting for, freaks? Come and get it!" As the man in black shouted, the heads of nearly half of the fang-baring villagers closing in on him from all sides went sailing into the air, sliced cleanly like so many watermelons.

An instant later, silver light limned another corona, and the heads flew from the next rank. Even novice vampires like these knew they mustn't lose their heads or brains, but they dropped to the ground leaking gray matter or spouting bloody geysers as if they were fountainheads.

What had severed the heads of the vampire victims so cleanly was one of the blades that'd hung at the man's waist. The blades were about a foot in diameter and shaped like a half-moon. Honed to a razor-fine arc, the weapon was known among the warriors of the Frontier as the crescent blade. A wire or cord was usually affixed to one end, and the wielder could set up a sort of safety zone around himself, keeping his enemies at bay by spinning the blade as widely or tightly as he wished. Due to the intense training necessary to handle it, there were few who could use one effectively.

But now, the weapons swished from both hands of the man in black to paint gorgeous silver arcs, slashing through villagers like magic—to the right and the left, above him and below, never missing the slightest change in their position. In fact, each and every one of the villagers had clearly been cut from a different angle. His lightning-speed attacks came from phantasmal angles. It didn't seem possible that anything he set his sights on would be spared.

Another particularly weird sound, entirely different from the slice of the crescent blade, came from his companion's favorite weapon—the hexagonal staff that was always on his back. Both ends had sharp protrusions, veritable stakes, but normally this weapon would be spun and used to bludgeon opponents. Its owner was using the hexagonal staff in this manner. However, the way that he swung the staff was unique. Spinning it around his waist like a water wheel set on its side, he smashed in the head of a foe to his right, spun it clear around his back, and took out an opponent to his left. The movement took less than a tenth of a second.

In a snap, four shadowy figures hung in the air to the left and the right of the man with the hexagonal staff, and before and behind him as well. This leaping assault capitalized on the superhuman strength unique to vampires.

The man with the hexagonal staff struck the first blow. His movements were sheer magic.

An instant after he staved in the hoary head of the old man to his right, the old woman before him went sailing through the air with her bottom jaw knocked clear off. With almost no delay, the two to his left and behind him were both speared through the heart by the tips of his staff.

What kind of strength did this ungodly display demand? Actually, the man with the hexagonal staff had his right arm stock still up around the shoulder. To all appearances, his right hand from the wrist down didn't quiver or move, and the staff seemed to spin of its own accord, giving the impression of smashing the villagers all by itself.

It wasn't humanly possible.

Still, the villagers numbered five hundred. Even with the skills this pair had, they couldn't keep the vampires from attacking the bus. In fact, the other vampires ignored the two of them and pounded across the ground in a dash for the vehicle.

And every time the wind howled, a number of them screamed and dropped in unison. The wind roared, and villagers fell like beads from a string, only to be skewered together again by arrows from the giant's bow.

The bow itself wasn't the kind of finished good you'd find for sale in city shops. It was a savage thing, just a handy low-hanging branch that'd been snapped off and strung with the gut of some beast. Even the contents of the quivers strapped to both of the giant's flanks and his back were no more than simple iron rods filed to a point.

But in the hands of this giant, they became missiles of unrivaled accuracy.

The giant didn't use them one at a time. Drawing back five at once, he released the arrows simultaneously. The acts of both getting the arrows out and then nocking them off seemed to be simplicity itself. Judging from his speed, he seemed to just be shooting wildly, without taking aim.

And yet, not a single arrow missed the mark. Not only did they not miss, but each arrow pierced the hearts of at least three villagers. This was only the natural way to attack, given that vampires wouldn't die by being run through the stomach, but the question was, how could the giant choose a target and move his bow in less time than it took to blink?

This remained a mystery even as the villagers left corpse upon corpse heaped before the bus.

It was then that a small shriek arose from behind the mounted men. They heard a woman's voice coming from inside the bus.

"That ain't good. Fall back!"

Before the giant had shouted the words, the men were whipping around toward the bus behind them.

With a bestial snarl, the villagers started to run. When the rapidly dwindling distance shrunk to a mere fifteen feet, the ground-pounding feet of the fiends came to an unexpected halt.

A lone youth suddenly stood between them and the bus, blocking them.

But it was not that alone that stopped the rush of these bloodthirsty creatures. For starters, there was the question of where this youth had appeared from.

With the gentle wave in the forelock touching his brow, the youth's face was strong and had a healthy tone, and, from the center of it his innocent eyes gazed at the hell-spawn without a hint of fear.

The villagers, who'd hesitated due to the way the youth unexpectedly appeared, must have deemed him the most desirable of prey. An instant later they were pressing forward toward him, as a single tide.

And then something happened.

Into the darkness were born a number of streaks of light.

Like silvery fish that burst flying through the waves, the lights looked as chaotic as cloth whipped by a high wind, but their accuracy was truly peerless, for each individual flash lanced through the hearts of countless villagers. Five hundred vampires hit in an instant . . . Flames spouting from their chests, the villagers fell. Writhing, then stiffening, the peaceful faces that came with death were surely the ones they'd had until dusk of the day before, returning to them now as serene masks.

From the cover of the bus, the man with the hexagonal staff slowly showed his face. Seeing the corpses lying in heaps, he said, "Wow, pretty damn intense," then gave an appreciative whistle. Once he'd whistled, he looked up at one of the windows on the bus and asked, "Is good ol' Grove doing all right?" His expression showed concern.

He didn't even glance at the young man who'd done all this. That man had already vanished. Every bit as mysteriously as he'd appeared.

"It couldn't be helped, and what's done is done," the man in black said, coming around from the other side. "We've got bigger fish to fry. The geezer said the Noble that grabbed his daughter took off to the north, right? If we go now, we could definitely catch up to 'em, bro. We could track 'em, run 'em down. Ten million if we bring her back safe. Sure he's probably already had his way with her, but what the hell, we'd be dealing with a woman on the other end. We could threaten her, tell her we chopped the girl's head off along with the vampire's, and turned her back into a human. She'd keep her trap shut and pay up."

Behind him, the giant muttered, "That'd all be well and good, if he'd been talking to us."

"What do you mean?"

The man in black looked at the giant's face, then followed the giant's line of sight toward the thicket ahead of them and off to the right. Earlier, that was the same spot the old man had addressed when he spoke.

"Come on out!"

As the giant said this, a crescent blade in the man in black's right hand gleamed in the moonlight, and the hexagonal staff ripped through the wind.

They, too, had known that this unearthly miasma hadn't belonged to the old man. The one responsible for it was in the woods. Their hands went to their weapons. The aura coming from the thicket gave them the same chill that radiated from the Nobility. They grasped their weapons fiercely, wanting to conceal their humiliation at not having uncovered the source of those emanations.

"If you don't come out, we're coming in, but from the way that old man was talking to you, I'm guessing we've gotta be in the same line of work. Hell, it seems you're even more dependable than we are. If that's the case, we don't wanna do nothing stupid. What do you say we talk this ten million deal out all friendly-like?" The giant waited a while after finishing his proposal. There was no answer, nor any movement. His thick, caterpillar-like eyebrows hoisted up quickly.

"Bro, this way's a lot quicker."

The crescent blade flew from the hand of the man in black. While it wasn't clear what it was constructed of, it wove through the trees, speeding to the spot at which the giant glowered. It was an assault devoid of ceremony, but steeped in murderous intent.

There was a beautiful sound. A silver flash of light coursed back out between the trees.

Behind the two men who yelped and jumped out of the way there was the sound of steel cleaving darkness.

What the giant now grasped in his right hand was the same crescent blade the man in black had just unleashed. A red band was slowly running down its finely honed surface. Fresh blood poured from the giant's hand. The emotional hue welling up on that rock-like face was one of fury, and also one of fright.

"Not bad," said the man with the hexagonal staff, giving a kick to his horse's flanks.

The horse didn't move.

Once again he kicked. His boots had spurs on the heels. The hide on the flanks broke, and blood trickled out. And yet still the horse didn't move.

When he noticed it was thoroughly cowed, the man with the hexagonal staff finally stopped giving the horse his spurs.

The door of the bus opened. A girl stuck her head out and asked, "What's going on, guys?" Acutely sensitive to the presence there, her beautiful face turned automatically to the depths of the woods. Imitating her older brothers.

In the depths of the darkness, the presence stirred. The clop of hooves drew steadily closer.

Suddenly the youth was before them, bathed in moonlight. It was as if the darkness itself had crystallized and taken human form.

II

Mysterious as the sparkle of the blue pendant shining from the breast of his black coat was, it ranked a distant second to the gorgeous visage that showed below the traveler's hat.

Astride his horse with the reins in his fist, the beautiful youth seemed as calm as any traveler passing through by happenstance, but one look at him and it was clear he was far from being a mere traveler.

"What the hell are you supposed to be?" the man in black asked in a thick, lethargic tone. The traveler's good looks were enough to send chills down his spine. That, combined with the knowledge that this guy had just batted back his lethal attack, made him speak in this strange voice.

The shadowy figure didn't answer. He moved forward, seemingly intent on casually breezing past them.

"Hold up," the man with the hexagonal staff shouted in an attempt to stop him. "Look, buddy, you might be one of the Hunters that geezer called, but so are we. Sure, we might've been in the wrong flying off and taking a poke at you like that, but there's no harm in us all introducing ourselves. We're the Marcus clan—I'm Nolt, the second oldest of the boys."

The shadowy figure halted his advance.

"This here's Kyle, the youngest brother," Nolt continued.

Eyes gleaming with animosity, the man in black made no attempt at a greeting.

"The great big fella is our older brother Borgoff."

Just as his brother finished introducing him, a sharp sound came from around the giant's thigh. The crescent blade, now in two pieces, fell to the ground with a shower of glittering silver flecks. The unusual break in it was not from folding. It was from squeezing. The giant wiped his bloody palm on his horse's ear. Blood stuck to the creature's coat, forcing the hair to fall in a mat.

"We've got another brother, but he's sick and doesn't get out of our ride. And finally, there's Leila, our baby sister."

"Nice to meet you, Mr. Tight-lips." Behind that oh-so-amiable voice, Leila's bright feline eye burned with flames of hostility. However, when the face of the traveler made a rapid turn in her direction, those flames suddenly wavered.

"The Marcus clan—I've heard of you," the traveler said, speaking for the first time. Without inflection, his voice was like iron, devoid of all possible emotion. The voice didn't match his incredibly good looks, but then again, no other voice would have been more appropriate.

However, the fact that he spoke in such a tone even after learning the names of these men . . .

The Marcus clan was the most skillful vampire hunting group on the Frontier. Consisting of five members, the family from oldest to youngest was Borgoff, Nolt, Groveck, Kyle, and Leila. The number of Nobles they'd taken care of reached triple digits, and word of how, miraculously, none of the clan had been lost in the process circulated far and wide among the people of the Frontier.

At the same time, so did tales of the clan's cruelty and callousness.

Nowhere did it say only one Vampire Hunter or group of Hunters could be hired for a given case. Considering the vengeance the Nobility would wreak in the event of failure, it was perfectly normal for the person concerned to employ a number of individuals, or even several groups.

The Marcus clan always lasted until the very end. They alone. No individual or group that had worked with them, or against them for that matter, had ever survived.

Due to the fact that none of the other Hunters' corpses had ever been recovered, there was no choice but to believe the Marcuses' claims that the Hunters were slain by the Nobility, but rumors spread like wildfire, and now an ominous storm of suspicion swirled over the clan members' heads.

Be that as it may, no one doubted their abilities as Hunters. After all, the number of Nobility their group had single-handedly destroyed was staggering.

Still, when other Hunters heard the Marcuses' name, the abhorrence felt was always coupled with a sense of aweover the threat the other killers felt from the clan's clearly demonstrated ability, and their willingness to use their skills for harm.

In all likelihood, this was probably the first time the clan had ever heard a man say their name so calmly.

"Look, jerk—" Unexpectedly, the giant—Borgoff—made a strange face. "—er, pal . . . I've heard about someone with your looks and a blue pendant. Ten years back, this one village elder told us there was only one Hunter in all the Frontier that was a match for us. That alone he was probably tougher than all of us put together or some such thing . . . But you couldn't be . . . "

Giving no answer, the young man turned away, as if completely unconcerned by the bunch of fearsome villains in front of him.

"Uh, hey, wait up," the man with the hexagonal staff called out. "We're going after the Noble that grabbed the geezer's daughter. If you're not with us, that makes you an enemy, too. Is that the way you want it?"

There was no response, and the horse and rider's silhouette was swallowed by the darkness.

"We're not gonna let him go, are we?" Leila asked indignantly, but Borgoff didn't seem to be listening,

"A dhampir . . . is that what he is then . . . ?" he muttered with an imbecilic look on his face. This was the first time the younger siblings had heard the man speak in such a tone.

Or say a certain, mysterious name.

"I've finally met a man I actually fear . . . D."

†

The spot was thirty miles north of the village of Vishnu, where wholesale slaughter followed tragedy in just two short days.

A lone black carriage rushed along the narrow road through the forest. The six horses that pulled it were ebon, too, and the driver in the coachman's perch was garbed in black. The whole vehicle seemed born of the darkness.

Showering the horses with merciless lashes, the driver occasionally looked to the heavens.

The sky was so full of stars it seemed to be falling. Their light seemed to flicker on the face gazing up at them. The graceful visage of the driver clouded suddenly.

"The stars moved. Those giving chase . . . to me . . . Six of them." There in the darkness, his eyes began to give off a blazing light. "And no mere pursuers at that . . . Each possessed of extraordinary skill . . . One of them in particular . . . "

As if unable to contain his agitation, he stood upright in the coachman's perch, shaking the jet-black vehicle beneath his feet.

"I won't let them have her. I won't let anyone take her away." Light coursed from the eyes he opened wide. Blood light.

There was a sudden discordance in the monotonous drone of the carriage wheels.

When turbulence had raced into that graceful face, one of the right wheels slipped off the axle with a crash. The wind groaned and the carriage lurched wildly to the right, kicking up a thick cloud of dust as the carriage rolled over.

What was truly unbelievable was the acrobatics of the driver. Releasing the reins of his own accord, sailing through the air, and skillfully twisting his body, he regained his balance, landing like a length of black cloth a few yards from the carriage.

Anxiety and despair filled his face as he dashed to the vehicle.

Throwing the door open like a man possessed, he peered inside. His anxiety was replaced by relief.

Letting out a deep sigh, he approached the special metal-alloy wagon-wheel that lay some thirty feet away.

"So, misfortune has decided to put in an unfashionably early appearance," he muttered glumly, lifting the wheel and walking back to the carriage. He looked to the sky once again. In a low voice, he said, "Soon the day will be breaking. Seems I shall be walking to the Shelter, and repairing this when it's night again. That's more than enough time for those dogs to catch up to us."

†

Around the time the mountain ridges were rising faintly from the darkness like the edges of so many jigsaw pieces, the pair halted their horses. They were atop a fair-sized hill.

"Ol' Borgoff's got us doing some crazy shit—riding hard in the middle of the night like this. I tell you, he's all worked up over nothing," the man in black said, giving a light wave of his right hand. The green grass below him was shaken by a dye deeper than the darkness.

In the pale, panting darkness of daybreak, this man alone seemed blackly clad in the remnants of night. In a black shirt and pants, it was Kyle—the youngest of the Marcus boys. The ebon flecks that remained like stains not just on his right hand but on his chest and shoulder as well were splashes of blood from all the nocturnal beasts they'd cut down during their ride.

"I thought he told you to stow that talk. That punk—he's no garden-variety Hunter. You must've heard about him, too," the man said in an attempt to settle his wild younger brother, a black staff looming on his back. The man speaking was Nolt, the second oldest.

"Ha! You mean how he's a dhampir?" Kyle spat the words. "A lousy *half-breed*, part Nobility and part human. Oh, sure, everyone says they make the best Vampire Hunters, don't they? But let's not forget something. We slaughter real, full-blooded Nobles!"

"Hey, you've got a point there."

"If he's a half-breed, he's more like us than the Nobility. Nothing to be afraid of. Not to mention, we even rode all night just so he wouldn't lose us, but if you ask me our big brother's lost his nerve. Who besides us would race through a Frontier forest in the middle of the night on horseback?"

Out on the Frontier, the forests were thick with monsters by night.

Though it was true the beasts' numbers had decreased with the decline of the Nobility, to move through the woods before dawn you still either had to be a complete idiot, or someone endowed with nerves of steel and considerable skill. As the brothers were.

It was for this reason Kyle was repulsed by the oldest of the boys, who'd ordered their charge by night so that the youth they'd met earlier wouldn't get a lead on them. Even he would be set upon by numerous creatures before he made it to this hill. The only reason they'd somehow managed to get there before daybreak was because they'd passed through the area before and knew a shortcut through the woods.

"Well, I don't know about that," Nolt said wryly, being more philosophical than the youngest boy. "We're talking about a guy that fended off your crescent blade, after all."

While Kyle glared at the second oldest, Nolt's eyes glimmered. "A horse—I wouldn't have thought it possible."

Kyle was at a loss for words. Sure enough, the sound of iron-shod hoofs came from the depths of the same forest from which the two brothers had just emerged. "It was no problem for us because we knew a shortcut. But that son of a bitch . . ."

Just as the two were exchanging glances, a horse and rider appeared from part of the forest below them, knifing through the darkness. Making a smooth break for the road, the figure struck them as being darker than the blackness.

"It's him all right," said Nolt.

"He ain't getting away," Kyle shot back.

There was a loud smack at the flanks of the pair's mounts, and hoofs were soon kicking up the sod.

With intense energy, they pursued the black-clad silhouette. The way he raced, he seemed a demon of the night, almost impossible to catch.

"We got orders from Borgoff. Don't try nothing funny." Nolt's voice flew at Kyle's back, about a horse-length ahead of him.

They couldn't have D getting ahead of them, but, even if it looked like that might happen, they weren't to do anything rash. Borgoff had ordered them not to attack in the sternest tone they'd ever heard from him.

But for all that, the flames of malice burned out of control in Kyle's breast. It wasn't simply that he had the wildest and most atrocious nature of all his siblings. His lethal crescent blade attack had been warded off by D. For a young man with faith in strength alone, that humiliation was intolerable. What he felt toward D surpassed hatred, becoming nothing less than pure, murderous intent.

Kyle's right hand went for the crescent blade at his waist.

However . . . the two of them couldn't believe their eyes. They just couldn't catch up.

They should have been closing the gap on the horse and rider who didn't seem to be going any faster than they were, but weren't they in fact rapidly falling farther and farther behind?

"Sonuvabitch!" Kyle screamed. Even as he put more power behind the kicks to his horse, his foe still dashed away, the tail of his black coat fluttering in the breeze he left. In no time at all, he shrunk to the size of a pea and vanished from their field of view.

"Dammit. Goddamn freak!"

Giving up and bringing his horse to a halt, Kyle trained his flaming pupils on the point in the road that had swallowed the shadowy figure.

"We ride all night, only to have this happen in the end . . . " Nolt said bitterly. "From the looks of it, we're never gonna catch up to him by normal means. Let's wait here for Borgoff to show up."

III

Around him, the wind swirled.

His hair streamed out, and the wide brim of the traveler's hat seemed to flow like ink. The silver flecks crumbling dreamlike against his refined brow and graceful nose were moonlight. Though the air already wore a tinge of blue, the moonlight reflected in his gaze shone as brightly as in the blackest of nights. While it was possible for a specially modified cyborg horse to gallop at an average speed of about sixty miles per hour, the speed of this horse put that to shame.

What could you say about a rider who could work such magic on the kind of standard steed you might find anywhere?

The road dwindled into the distant flatness of the plain.

Without warning, the rider pulled back on the reins. The horse's forequarters twisted hard to the right, while the sudden stop by the forelegs kicked up gravel and dirt. This rather intense method of braking was not so much mesmerizing as it was mildly unsettling. Once again, the moonlight fell desolately on the rider's shoulders and back.

Without a sound, the black-clad figure dismounted. Bending down, he patiently scrutinized lines in the dirt and gravel, but he soon stood upright and turned his face toward the nearby stand of trees. This person, possessed of such intense beauty as to make the moonlight bashful to be around him, was none other than D.

"So, this is where they left the usual route then. What's he up to?" Muttering this in a way that didn't seem a question at all, he mounted his horse again and galloped toward the tree line.

All that remained after he vanished through the trees was the moonlight starkly illuminating the narrow road, and the distant echo of fading hoofbeats.

The moon alone knew that some six hours earlier a driver in black coming down the road had changed the direction of his carriage in that very spot. Had D discerned the tracks of the carriage he sought, picking them out from all the ruts left by the number of electric buses and other vehicles that passed this way by day?

Shortly thereafter, the moon fused with the pale sky, and, in its place, the sun rose.

Before the sun got to the middle of the sky, D and his steed, who'd been galloping all the while, broke out of another in an endless progression of forests and halted once again.

The ground before him had been wildly disturbed. This was the spot where the carriage had lost a wheel and rolled.

Starting out a full twenty-four hours late, D had caught up in half a day. Of course, it was the fate of the Nobility to sleep while the sun was high, and the Marcus clan was still far behind. The speed and precision of the pursuit by the team of mount and rider was frightening.

But where had the carriage gone?

Without getting off his horse, D glanced at the overturned soil, then gave a light kick to his mount's flanks.

They headed for the hill before them at a gradual pace, quite a change from the way they'd been galloping up to this point.

It was a mound of dirt that really couldn't be called a hill, but, standing atop it looking down, D's eyes were greeted by the sudden appearance of a structure that seemed quite out of place.

It looked like a huge steel box. With a width of more than ten feet and a length of easily thirty, its height was also in excess of ten feet. In the brilliant sunlight that poured down, the black surface threw off blinding flames.

This was the Shelter the Noble in black had mentioned.

Immortal though the vampires might be, they still had to sleep by day. While their scientific prowess had spawned various antidotes for sunlight, they never succeeded in conquering the hellish pain that came when their bodies were exposed to it. The agony of cells blazing one by one, flesh and blood putrefying, every bodily system dissolving—even the masters of the earth were still forced to submit to the legends of antiquity.

Though the vampires had reached the point where their bodies wouldn't be destroyed, many of the test subjects exposed to more than ten minutes of direct sunlight were driven insane by the pain; those exposed for even five minutes were left crippled, their regenerative abilities destroyed. And, no matter what treatment they later received, they never recovered.

But in the Nobility's age of prosperity, that had mattered little.

Superspeed highways wound to every distant corner of the Frontier, linear motor-cars and the like formed a transportation grid that boasted completely accident-free operation, and the massive energy-production facilities erected in and around the Capital provided buses and freight cars with an infinite store of energy.

And then the decline began.

At the hands of the surging tide of humanity, all that the Nobility had constructed was destroyed piece by piece, reducing their civilization to ruins hardly worthy of the name. Even the power plants with their perfect defense systems collapsed, a casualty of mankind's tenacious, millennia-spanning assault.

While the situation wasn't so dire in metropolitan areas, Nobility in the Frontier sectors were stripped of all means of transportation. Though there were many in the Nobility who'd expected this day would come and had established transportation networks in the sectors they controlled, they inevitably lost the enthusiasm and desire to maintain the networks themselves.

Even now, silver rails ran through prairies damp with the mists of dawn, and somewhere in colossal subterranean tunnels lay the skeletons of automated, ultra-fast hovercrafts.

Before carriages became the sole means of transportation, accidents caused by the failure of radar control and power outages occurred frequently.

To the humans, who'd learned how to use the scientific weapons of the Nobility or could penetrate the vehicular defenses with armaments they'd devised on their own, Nobles in transit and immobilized by day were the ideal prey.

Due to the intense demand from the Frontier, the Noble's government in the Capital—where the remaining power was concentrated—constructed special defensive structures at strategic locations along their transportation network.

These were the Shelters.

Though built from a steel-like plating only a fraction of an inch thick, the Shelters could withstand a direct hit from a small nuclear device, and there were a vast array of defensive mechanisms armed and ready to dispose of any insects who might be buzzing around with stakes and hammers in hand.

But what made these Shelters perfect, more than anything else, was one simple fact—

"There's no entrance?" D muttered from atop his horse.

Exactly. The jet-black walls that reflected the white radiance of the sun didn't have so much as a hair-sized crack.

Looking up at the heavens, D started silently down the hill.

The pleasant vernal temperature aside, the sunlight that ruthlessly scorched him was unparalleled agony for a dhampir like D. Dhampirs alone could battle with the Nobility on equal terms by night, but to earn the title of Vampire Hunter, they needed the strength to remain impassive in the blistering hell of the day.

As D drew closer, it seemed the surrounding air bore an almost imperceptible groaning, but that soon scattered in the sunlight.

At D's breast, his pendant glowed ever bluer. It was a mysterious hue that rendered all of the Nobility's electronic armaments inoperable.

Dismounting in front of the sheer, black wall, D put his left hand to the steel. A chilling sensation spread through him. The temperature was probably unique to this special steel. Perhaps it was because, to render the exterior of this structure impervious to all forms of heat or electronic waves, molecules served as atoms in it.

D's hand glided slowly across the smooth surface.

Finishing the front wall, he moved to the right side. It took thirty minutes to run his hand over that side.

"Sheesh," said a bored voice coming from the space between the steel and the palm of his hand. The voice let a sigh escape as D moved to the back wall. If there'd been anyone there to hear it, this bizarre little scene would've undoubtedly made the eyes bug out of their head, but D continued his work in silence.

"Yep, this metal sure is tough stuff. The situation inside is kind of hazy. Still, I'm getting a picture of the general setup. The superatomic furnace inside is sending energy into the metal itself. You can't break through the walls without destroying the atomic furnace, but in order to do that you'd have to bust through the walls first. So, which came first, the chicken or the egg?"

"How many are inside?" D asked, still brushing his hand along the wall.

"Two," came the quick reply. "A man and a woman. But even I can't tell whether they're Nobility or human."

Without so much as a nod, D finished scanning the third wall.

Only the left side remained.

But what in the world was he doing? Judging from what the voice said, he seemed to be searching the interior of the Shelter, but, if the outer walls couldn't be breached, that was pointless. On the other hand, the voice explained that destroying the outer walls would be impossible.

About halfway down the steel wall, the left hand halted.

"Got it," the voice said disinterestedly.

D wasted no time going into action. Without taking his left hand away, he stepped back, reaching with his right for his sword. The blade seemed to drink up the sunlight.

Drawing his sword-wielding right arm far back, D focused his eyes on a single point on the wall. A spot right between the thumb and forefinger of his left hand.

But what had they got there? The instant an awesome white bloodlust coalesced between the naked sword tip and the steel—

A pale light pierced the black wall.

It was D's sword that streamed forth. Regardless of how trenchant that thrust might be, there was no way it could penetrate the special steel of the outer walls. Be that as it may, the graceful arc sank halfway into the unyielding metal wall.

That's where the entrance was. D's blade was wedged in the boundary between door and wall, though that line was imperceptible to the naked eye. With the mysterious power of his left hand D had located it, then thrust into it. Granted that there was a space there, how could the tip of his sword slip into an infinitesimal gap?

"Wow!" The voice that said this came not from the interior, but rather from D's left hand. "Now here's a surprise. One of them's human."

D's expression shifted faintly. "Do they have Time-Bewitching Incense?" he asked. That was a kind of incense the Nobility had devised to give day the illusion it was night.

"I don't know, but the other one's not moving. A dead man, at least by day."

"The girl's okay then?" D muttered. Most likely she'd been bitten at least once, but if that were the case, destroying the one responsible would restore her humanity. Why then did a dark shadow skim for an instant across D's features?

The muscles of the hand he wrapped around the hilt bulged slowly. It's unclear what kind of exquisite skill was at work, but the slightest twist of the horizontal blade sent a sharp, thin line racing across the steel surface.

Blue light oozed out.

D immediately ceased all activity. Silently, he turned his face to the rear. His cold pupils were devoid of any hue of emotion.

"Earlier than I expected," the voice said, as if it were mere banter. "And not who I expected at all."

Presently, the faint growl of an engine came from the forest, and then a crimson figure leapt over the crest of the hill.

Raising a cacophony, a single-seat battle car stopped right at the bottom of the slope.

The vehicle was an oblong iron plate set on four grotesquely oversized, puncture-proof tires. The vehicle was crammed with a high-capacity atomic engine and some controls. The product of humans who'd got their hands on some of the Nobility's machinery, its outward appearance was a far cry from what the average person might call aesthetically pleasing. An energy pipe with conspicuous welding marks twisted like a snake from the rear-mounted engine to a core furnace shielded by studded iron-plate, and the simple bar-like steering yoke jutted artlessly from the floor. Churning in the air like the legs of a praying mantis, the pistons connected to the tires—and all the other parts, for that matter—were covered with a black grime, probably some harmless radioactive waste.

Perhaps what warranted more attention than the appearance of the vehicle were its armaments and its driver. Looming large from the right flank of the rear-mounted engine was the barrel of a 70 mm recoilless bazooka, staring blackly at D, while on the other side, the left, a circular, 20 mm missile pod glowered at empty space. Naturally, the missiles were equipped with body-heat seekers, and naught save certain death awaited the missiles' prey. And finally, ominously mounted atop the core furnace and exhibiting a muzzle that looked like it had a blue jewel set in the middle of it, was the penetrator—a cannon with grave piercing power.

Yet, despite the fact that it had a lot of heavy equipment not found on the average battle car, judging from the size of the core furnace and engine, this vehicle could easily be pressed for speeds of seventy-five miles per hour. It would run safely on ninety-nine percent of all terrain, and, thanks to its three-quarter-inch thick wire suspension, it could be driven on even the worst of roads. It raced across the ground, a miniature behemoth.

A figure in crimson rose from the driver's seat and jerked a pair of sturdy goggles off. Blue eyes that seemed ablaze took in D. Blonde hair lent its golden hue to the wind. It was Leila, the younger sister of the Marcus clan.

"So, we meet again," said the girl.

Perhaps it was the animosity radiating from every inch of her that made her vermilion coverall seem to blaze in the daylight. Her body, jolting to the incessant groaning of the engine, seemed to twitch with loathing for D.

"You might've thought you beat my older brothers just fine, but as long as I'm around you can't steal a march on the Marcus clan. Seems I ran into you at just the right spot. Is my prey in there?" This girl referred to the Nobility as her prey. She spat the words with a self-confidence and hostility that was beyond the pale.

D continued to stand as still as a sculpture, sword in hand.

"Out of my way," Leila said, in a tone she used for giving orders. "It was unfortunate for my prey that they had nothing but this broken Shelter, and fortunate for you, but now I'll be taking that good fortune, thank you. If you value your life, you'd best turn tail now."

"And if I don't value it, what'll you do?"

D's soft voice caused a reddish hue every bit as vivid as her raiment to shoot into her face.

"How's that? You seriously want to tangle with Leila Marcus and her battle car?"

"I have two lives. Take whichever one you like. That is, if you can."

The serene voice, unchanged since the first time she heard it, made Leila fall silent. The tomboy hesitated.

She hadn't realized yet that the blade piercing the wall of the Shelter was there due to D's secret skill alone. From the very start, it never crossed her mind that anything alive could perform such a feat. Still unaware of D's true power, Leila's hesitation was born of movements in her heart to which she was as yet oblivious.

The man in black standing before her left her feeling shockingly numbed. Like a mysterious drug, his presence worked like an anesthetic that violated her to the very marrow of her bones. As if to strip the movement from her heart, Leila roughly jerked her goggles back down.

"That's too bad. This is the way we Marcuses do it!" Just as the crimson coverall settled back in the driver's seat, the engine howled. She'd purposely cut the muffler to antagonize her opponents. The instant her hands took the controls, the massive tires flattened the grass. Not so much coming down the hill, the battle car was closer to flying, and her wheels kicked up the earth even as it touched back down. In less than a tenth of a second it'd taken off again. Its speed didn't seem possible from a mechanical construct.

It made a mad rush straight for D.

D didn't move.

A terrible sound shook the air, now mixing with a fishy stench. The smell was accompanied by smoke. White smoke billowing from the burnt tires, the vehicle stopped just inches short of D.

"You're gonna feel this to the bone. Here I come!" Leila's hysterical shouts were just another attempt to conceal the uneasiness of her own heart. The foot that had floored the gas to run down D had hit the brake a hair's breadth from crushing him. But why hadn't D moved? It was as if he'd read the ripples spreading through her chest.

Without saying a word, he pulled back on his stuck sword. It came free all too quickly. Sheathing it without a sound in a single fluid movement, D turned.

"I thought you'd see it my way. You should've done that from the get-go. Could've saved us both some trouble by not trying to act so damn tough." Leila kept her eyes on D until he'd climbed the hill and disappeared over the summit. An instant later, tension drew her feline eyes tight.

With a low groan, the earth shook violently. Though it weighed over a ton, the battle car was tossed effortlessly into the air, smashed into the ground, and was tossed up again.

Now that D had gone, the Shelter's defense systems sprang into action.

Though it looked impossible to steady, Leila stood impassively in her car. She had one hand on the yoke, but that was all. She remained perpendicular to the car throughout its crazed dance, as if the soles of her feet were glued to the floorboards.

In midair, Leila took her seat.

The engine made a deafening roar. Blue atomic flames licked from the rear nozzles, and smoke from the spent radioactive fuel flew from exhaust pipes off the engine's sides. The battle car took off in midair.

As it touched down, the penetrator over the engine swiveled to point at the Shelter. Unhindered by the wildly rocking earth, bounding with each shock, still the car never lost its bearing.

The air was stained blue.

The ceiling of the Shelter opened, and a laser cannon reminiscent of a radar dish appeared and spurted out a stream of fire. It skimmed the airborne body of the car and reduced a patch of earth to molten lava.

If this weapon was radar-controlled, then there was certainly cause to be alarmed. The second and third blasts of fire, usually vaunted for their unmatched precision, flew in vain, as their target slipped in front or behind, to the left or right of where they fell.

Leila's skill behind the wheel surpassed these electronic devices.

As far back as she could remember, the clan's father had always impressed upon her how important it was for her to refine her skills at manipulating anything and everything mechanical. Her father may have even known some basic genetic enhancement techniques.

Ironically, Leila's talents only seemed to shine when it came to modes of transportation. Whether it was a car, or even something with a life of its own like a cyborg horse, under her skillful touch mechanical vehicles were given a new lease on life. "Give her an engine and some wheels and she'll whip up a car," her father had said with admiration. Her skill at operating vehicles surpassed that of all her brothers, with only the oldest boy Borgoff even coming close.

And how Leila loved her battle car. It had been crafted from parts gathered in junkyards during their travels. Some parts even came from the ruins of the Nobility, when the opportunity to take them presented itself. She'd quite literally forgotten to eat or sleep while she worked on it. Early one winter morning, the battle car was completed by the feeble, watery light of dawn. Two years had passed since then. Loving that car like a baby that'd kicked in her own belly, Leila learned to drive it with a miraculous level of skill.

The very epitome of that skill was being displayed out on this hill-hemmed patch of ground. Avoiding every attack by the electronic devices, the vehicle changed direction in midair, and, just as the laser's fraction-of-a-second targeting delay was ending, the penetrator discharged a silvery beam.

It was a form of liquid metal. Expelled at speeds in excess of Mach 1, the molecular structure of the metal altered, changing to a five-yard-long spear that shot right through the workings of the laser cannon. Sending electromagnetic waves out in all directions like tentacles, the laser was silenced. As she brought the penetrator's muzzle to bear on one wall of the Shelter, a bloody smile rose on Leila's lips.

Suddenly, her target blurred. Or more accurately, the car sank. As if the land surrounding the Shelter had become a bog, the car sunk nose first into the ground.

Leila's tense demeanor collapsed, deteriorating into devil-may-care laughter.

The rear nozzles pivoted with a screech, disgorging fire. Flames ran along the sides of the vehicle, blowing away the rocky soil swallowing its muzzle. The tires spun at full speed. Whipping up a trail of dust, the battle car took to the air tail first. It spun to face the hill even before it touched back down, and the penetrator's turret swiveled to the back, hurling a blast of silver light against the Shelter wall.

The blast broke in two, and, in the same instant, was reduced to countless particles of light that flew in all directions. Even Leila's driving skills couldn't get her through this web of shrapnel.

However . . .

Landing back on solid ground, the battle car kept going straight for the storm of metallic particles, its body at a wild tilt as it pulled a wheelie. The darkness-shredding bullets sank into the belly of the car.

Giving the engine full throttle, Leila pushed her vehicle to the top of the hill in one mad dash.

Fugitives

CHAPTER 2

I

A s Leila hit the brakes, a gorgeous figure in black greeted her. "Very nicely done," D said in his serene tone.

Weathering a sensation that was neither fever nor chills racing down her spine, Leila replied with bald-faced hostility. "You still kicking around? If you don't make tracks and fast, I'm gonna have to run you down and kill you," she warned.

Without acknowledging her threat, D said softly, "Someone should take a look at your wound."

"And you'd best . . . mind your own business!" Pain spread through the last words Leila spat. Pressing a hand to her right breast, she toppled forward in the driver's seat. She'd taken a hit in the chest from a hunk of shrapnel that'd punched through the battle car's floorboards.

Walking over swiftly, D lifted Leila with ease and set her down in the shade of a nearby tree. Throwing a quick glance at the sky and the Shelter, D listened in the direction from which Leila had come.

"They're not coming," the palm of his left hand could be heard to say. "Her people are still a long way off. What are you planning on doing?"

"Can't leave her like this."

"You can play nursemaid to the mortally wounded later. Our target's in that steel box right now, completely immobilized. I say finish him off as soon as possible, and deliver the girl. After all, even if she's been bitten already, if we slay the Noble she'll be back to normal. That should please her no end."

Shrouded as always in an eerie aura, D's beautiful visage clouded for an instant. "She'd be pleased? Because she was human again? Or because he was—"

"Don't start harping on that again. Has this fine spring day knocked a few of your screws loose? We're so close, and if you just go do it now you could kill him without working up a sweat. The sun'll be setting soon, you know. I say let the competition rot." As if to corroborate the voice's growing impatience, the sky began to don a darker shade of blue. At this time of year, sunset came around five Night, which gave D fewer than two hours to finish his work.

Despite that, D pulled open the front of Leila's coverall without a word. Evident even through her clothing, the pale fullness of her bosom was now laid bare. The flesh above her left breast burst outwards in a number of spots. Already the bloodied wounds had swollen black and blue. They were like so many eerie sarcomata growing from her white skin.

D stood up, lifted the emergency kit from his saddlebags, and returned. When he opened the lid of the kit, agitation surged into his eyes.

"Heh heh heh," the voice cackled mockingly. "I was just trying to remember when you bought that set. You've been hauling it around all this time and never used it once. Well, the stuff inside became useless a long, long time ago. That's the trouble with *people who can't die*."

"Too true," D muttered in his usual monotone, doing a check of Leila's battle car and pulling out a first-aid kit. Just to be safe, he set it on the floorboards to open it, then closed it again quickly.

"What is it?"

"There's nothing in there. She's pretty much out of everything."

"So, didn't restock it, eh? Never heard of such a cavalier Hunter."

Wounds, you could say, were an occupational hazard for Hunters, and replacing medical supplies was every bit as important as procuring weapons. On arriving in a town or village, it was second nature for a Hunter to race to the arms merchant and pharmacy first, then hit the general store or saloon later.

But Leila had no medical supplies. And yet she was the youngest sister of the Marcus clan, whose five members ranked up there with a handful of veteran Hunters.

Once again D squatted by the girl's side.

Her breathing was rather shallow. Though it seemed the fragments within her hadn't damaged any internal organs, there was some danger of toxins from the shrapnel causing tetanus if the chunks of metal were left where they were. In fact, the entry and exit wounds were already swelling a deep, dirty red.

"What are you gonna do? You know I only work on you. Can't do a thing for humans."

"I know. There's no choice but to deal with humans the human way."

From the combat belt at his waist, D drew a caltrop. He brought one of the points to his left hand.

"What do you think you're doing?"

"If the girl dies, you and I are through."

"Shit. Are you threatening me?" But before the voice had finished speaking, pale blue flames enveloped the tip of the caltrop.

The sharp point heated quickly and turned crimson. D brought his left hand closer to Leila's brow. Her sizable eyes opened.

"What are you doing?" she asked.

"Cauterizing the wound. I'll do it so it doesn't hurt."

"How kind of you," she shot back sarcastically. "Don't expect me to thank you."

"Don't talk."

Leila jerked her face away from the approaching hand. "I don't know what kind of hocus-pocus you can pull, but I'll be damned if I'm gonna let you play around with my body while I'm out. I'm gonna be awake to see this from start to finish. Try anything funny, and believe me, you'll pay."

Undeterred, D set his left hand on her.

"Don't—" Leila's words became a scream. "Stop, I'm begging you. Do it while I'm still awake. Please," she pleaded.

Something glistening welled in her eyes as they gazed at D. It spoke of horrific memories.

Silently taking his hand away, D tore the sleeve of his coat and put a strip of cloth from it between Leila's lips. They had no anesthesia. The cloth was to keep her from biting her tongue. This time she cooperated quietly. The little nod she made must've been an expression of gratitude.

D lowered the hot metal to her skin. Shortly thereafter, a pungent scent and a series of low moans began to permeate the darkening bower.

†

D usk seemed to coalesce around him. He opened his eyes. Nothing could replace this feeling, that the spell that imprisoned him to the very last cell was drawing away like the tide. This was his favorite time.

His eyes hastened to his side. Not far from him, a girl sat quietly on the edge of the bed. She gave the impression of not having moved a muscle since she'd sat down. Her pretty white blossom of a face turned to him.

"What's wrong?" he asked, still lying flat on a bed littered with silk cushions. He'd glimpsed the trail of a teardrop on the girl's cheek.

"There's someone outside."

"Oh. Here already?" In the recesses of his tense voice lay unshakable self-confidence. Now matter how skilled the Vampire Hunter, nothing could match a Noble rising in darkness.

Stepping down lightly onto the steel floor, he glanced at the door and his eyes fairly shot out. Was that a threadlike silver line falling across the floor? Realizing that it was moonlight sneaking in through a crack carved above the door, he turned back to the girl.

"During the day, someone opened it with a sword," she said. "Hunters hired by Father, no doubt . . . "

Discerning a certain something on the blue dress that covered her down to the knees, he knit his brow. It was an elegant silver dirk. He'd been wearing it at his waist. What had she intended to use it for? For a brief while he focused on the weapon, then he made his way over to the video monitors on the wall to check on the situation outside.

†

By the time D had burned then carved away each wound, and had sterilized the damaged skin with a freshly heated caltrop, Leila finally passed out.

"For the most part her worries are over," the voice said. "But bacteria have already set up shop in her body. She'll be getting hit by some pretty intense chills soon. If she can get past that, she'll be able to rest easy. You've gone this far, might as well do the next step. Keep treating her through the home stretch."

With no sign of listening to the somewhat disgusted voice, D kept looking back and forth between the Shelter and the sky of ever-deepening blue. When the caltrop stuck in the ground had cooled he returned it to his belt and stood up, saying, "He should be coming out any minute now."

"You're so cold," the voice said with resentment. "You mean to tell me when he does, you'll just stop treating her? Don't run off like some back-alley quack." But then the voice stopped unexpectedly.

D took a step forward. Like stagnated blue light, the door to the Shelter retracted without a sound. Looking back, he saw Leila. The eyes that swiftly turned forward again held a lurid light. There he stood, the greatest Vampire Hunter of all. The hem of his coat fluttering in the night breeze, D came down the hill.

It wasn't long before the six obsidian horses appeared one after another—followed, of course, by the black lacquered carriage. Machinery within the Shelter had successfully completed the necessary repairs to it during the day.

A young man clad in black peered silently down at D from the coachman's perch. "Out of our way," he said. His voice was strangely soft. "Scum though you are for the way you place a price on people's lives, I still have no wish to engage in a pointless and lethal exchange."

An odd hue of emotion flowed into D's eyes, then swiftly vanished. "I'll take the girl," D said perfunctorily, his demeanor free from violence or exuberance.

The man's eyes were gradually being dyed red. "I took her because I want her," he said. "You should try to do the same. If you're up to battling a Noble at night, that is."

The darkness solidified. Though both the color and light remained the same there, the space between the two of them seemed to have suddenly frozen.

The crack of whipped flesh broke the stillness. Without even a whinny, two-dozen hooves began beating the earth. Whether their intent was to trample the insignificant Hunter or to make him get out of the way, those six madly charging horses unexpectedly came to a dead stop a few yards shy of D.

There was a startled cry of "Mayerling!"

The instant D realized the voice flew from a woman inside the carriage, his body soared into the air like a mystic bird. Still distracted by her plaintive cry, there was a split-second delay before D brought his silvery flash down at the youth's head.

Sparks spilled into the darkness like scattered jewels, trailing a beautiful metallic *ching* behind them. The youth—Mayerling—had stopped D's deadly stroke with the back of his left hand. That part of his hand was bound in steel armor.

Twisting his body out of the way of the three flashes of light roaring through the air toward his chest, D came silently back down to earth on the opposite side of the vehicle.

From the roof of the carriage down to D, the miasma flowed. And from D back up to the roof. At this intense exchange of unearthly auras, the horses whinnied, and the carriage rocked wildly.

Long claws grew from the fingers of the Noble's right hand. But no, they were not simply nails—glittering blackly, they clearly had the lustrous sheen of steel. When danger was near, the vampire's normal fingernails became murderous steel implements.

"Such a refined face, and such skill—I've heard your name before. The name that can make any Noble grow pale. So, you're D—" Mayerling said, his voice a blend of admiration and fear.

"I've heard of you, too," D responded softly. "I've heard there was a young lord praised for his virtue by his subjects, perhaps the only one among all the Nobility. His name was Mayerling, I'm quite certain."

"I always wanted to meet you. One way or another."

"Well, now you have," the Hunter replied. "I'm right here."

"Will you not let us go? I've done nothing to the humans."

"Tell that to the father you made like yourself before you carried off his daughter."

Distress filled Mayerling's countenance.

The tension abruptly drained from D's body.

With a shout of "Hyah!" from Mayerling, the horses pummeled the earth. Speeding by D's side, they started to gallop up the earthen slope.

D raced like the wind.

The carriage was every bit a match for D's speed.

At the summit of the hill, D came alongside the carriage. His right hand reached for the door handle. And then the golden handle just started pulling away. As he watched, the carriage dwindled in size, and D turned himself around and headed over to a stand of trees. That was where Leila lay.

"Heard a strange voice, didn't you?" the usual strange voice said. "Kinda makes you think being hard of hearing might not be so bad. We might be wrapping up this job right about now otherwise."

D squatted down and put a hand to Leila's brow. She was as hot as fire. Her sweat-drenched face was twisted with pain. Both fever and pain were due to her infection. Relentless chills would soon follow.

Without a moment's hesitation, D stripped off Leila's clothes. When her beautiful naked body was stretched out on the green grass, a surprised "Wow!" came from his left hand. "By the looks of it, I'd say this little girl's had a pretty hard life."

From her round, firm breasts down to her thighs, and across her whole back, Leila's skin was covered with the scars of numerous gashes and the stitches that had closed them. This was a girl who lived in the carnage that was the Frontier.

Without seeming to be harboring any strong emotion, D covered Leila with himself.

Crying out a little, Leila clung to his powerful chest. Her fever-swollen lips trembled, letting a mumbled word escape over and over again. A single word, but it was what had stayed D's hand at the carriage door.

†

When Kyle Marcus's mount crested the hill an hour later, there was no sign of anyone or anything in the vicinity, aside from his sister, who was wrapped in a blanket and resting peacefully in her seat in the battle car.

Another thirty minutes after that, the bus driven by Borgoff appeared, along with Nolt, who was riding point.

Kyle carried Leila into the vehicle in a great hurry. They must've been very close, because his expression had changed markedly. "She—she's gonna be okay, won't she, bro?" he stammered. "Give her something, I don't care what."

As Borgoff watched him struggle on the brink of tears, he wore a rancorous expression, but he took Leila's pulse nonetheless, checked her fever, and before long gave a satisfied nod. "She's all right. I'll check out her internal organs and circulation with a CAT scan anyway, but there's no need to worry." Staring down at Kyle where he'd slumped to the floor in apparent relief, he added, "This kinda shit is what happens when you go behind my back and send Leila out alone."

"I know. You can take the strap to me later for all I care. But which one of them you figure roughed Leila up so bad?"

Kyle's face had reclaimed its original viciousness. Eyes staring firmly into space, he was so angry he didn't notice the froth running from the corners of his mouth. His body shook.

"Well, probably not the one who treated her. Which means maybe it was neither of them. You wouldn't think anyone as soft as all that could survive this long out here on the Frontier."

"It don't matter," Kyle said, almost ranting deliriously. "It don't matter which of 'em did it. I'll find 'em both and cut 'em to pieces. Take their arms and legs off and put 'em back on where they don't belong. Stuff their mouths with their own steaming guts."

"Knock yourself out," his older brother said. "Anyway, you're sure there wasn't anyone around Leila? From the look of her wounds, she got them three, maybe four hours ago."

The door opened and Nolt stuck his head in. "We've got some tracks from a carriage passing this way. Still fresh. Maybe from an hour before we got here, tops. There's something else, too—some prints from horseshoes."

"If that's the case, then the two of them must've gone at it here, too. And it looks like it didn't get settled yet . . . "

Nodding gravely at his own words, Borgoff ordered Nolt to take care of Leila and Groveck. He went to his room in the back, returning to the driver's seat clutching a cloth-wrapped package of apparent significance.

"If I've seen D's face, I can spot him," he muttered, pulling from the cloth a silver disk about a foot and a half in diameter. Setting it up on a little stand almost in the center of the dashboard, Borgoff turned his heavily whiskered face to gaze out the window and up at the moon rising in the heavens. The moon was round and nearly full, but, thanks to the clouds obscuring part of it, it looked like it'd been nibbled here and there by bugs.

When he set his huge form down, the driver's seat creaked and groaned. Then Borgoff crossed his hands in front of his chest, and began to stare fixedly at the propped-up silver platter with eyes that looked like they could bore right through it. A minute passed, then two.

Kyle wouldn't leave Leila's side as she lay in bed. As Nolt peered in through the door next to the driver's seat sweat beaded his face just as profusely as Borgoff's.

And then, as the silvery surface of the platter grew smoky, almost like clouds covered it, the figure of a young man in black astride a horse suddenly formed on its surface.

It was D. Turning their way and saying something, he pulled on the reins in his hands and disappeared into a thicket.

It was a replay of D from the previous night, talking with them after the battle with the vampiric villagers. If people or things looked a little different, it was probably because these images were taken from Borgoff's memories. Here was a man who could project his own memories onto a silver platter. Yet, despite this admirable display of what some would call sorcery, Borgoff glared mercilessly at the moon in the sky with bloodshot eyes. No, not at the moon, but at a big mass of clouds under it. The moonlight shining on the clouds edged them in blue.

There was no change in either the moon or the cloud mass, or so it appeared for an instant. Then, even though the moon remained unchanged, the heart of the cloud mass seemed to begin to glow ever so faintly. In the space of a breath, a figure shaped like a man started wriggling there, and, with a second breath, it became a clear picture. Someone was riding a horse down a pitch-black road.

Based on his past memory of D, Borgoff was using the silver platter and moon as projectors to make the *present* D appear in the cloud mass.

The receding figure that seemed to be looking down on them from the distant heavens was a remarkable likeness of D as he raced down the road a few score miles ahead.

II

They'd run full tilt for a good two hours after leaving D in their dust, and, when Mayerling saw that the road continued on in a straight line for the next dozen or so miles, he left the coachman's perch of the racing carriage and skillfully slipped inside.

When he'd closed the door, not a hint of sound from the outside world intruded into the carriage. The girl sat there in a leather-bound chair like a night-blossoming moonbeam flower.

Carpet spread across the floor, and an exceedingly fine silk padding covered the walls and ceiling. In days of old, bottles of the best and rarest potables had sat on the collapsible golden table that seemed to grow from the wall, and this dozen miles of starlit road had run to great masquerades by the Nobility. However, the carpet was now somewhat dingy, there were tears in the silk, and there wasn't a single silver glass on the table. Even the table drooped for lack of a screw.

This model of carriage was said to be the last equipped with magnetic stabilizing circuits, which would hold the passengers safely in position even if the vehicle were to flip over.

Mayerling's right hand moved, and the interior was filled with light. "Why don't you turn on the lights?" he asked. "By rights this dilapidated old buggy should have been scrapped long ago, but that much at least is still operational."

Encouraged by a smile that bared teeth of limitless white, the girl showed Mayerling a smile in return. Yet her smile was thin, like a mirage.

He tried to recall the last time he'd seen this girl's brightly smiling face, but had little luck. Perhaps he'd only dreamt it, and was dreaming this as well.

"I don't mind," she replied. "If you live in the darkness, then I want to, too."

"I'm sure the sunlight suits you wonderfully. Though I have yet to see you in it," he added, heading over to the chair across from her to sit down.

"Do you think we'll make it all the way?" the girl asked hesitantly.

"You think we won't?"

"No." The girl shook her head. It was the first vehement action he'd seen from her since he'd taken her out of the village. "I'll be fine anywhere. So long as I'm with you, I could make my home in a cave in the craggy mountains or in some subterranean world where I'd never see the light of day again."

"No matter where we might be, the Hunters would come," he said, allowing resignation to drift into his jewel-like beauty. "Your fellow humans won't be happy until they've destroyed everything. You're nothing like them, of course."

She said nothing.

"There's nowhere on earth we can relax now. A long trip out into the depths of space . . . " He caught himself. "Perhaps it has become too much for you?"

"No."

"It's all right. Perhaps you weren't cut out for this from the very beginning. A graceful hothouse flower can't endure the ravages of the wild. You were kind enough to indulge my willfulness. We shall take a different course if you so desire."

The girl's white hand pressed down on his pale hand, and her slender face shook gently from left to right. "I want to try and see if we make it. To go to the stars."

Oh, who could have known the journey these two had undertaken was not a fiendish abduction, but rather a flight by a couple madly in love? A young vampire Nobleman and a human lass—linked not by fear and contempt, but by a bond of mutual love all the stronger for its hopelessness. Were that not the case, there was no chance this girl taken from a village where everyone had been turned into vampires would still be untainted, her skin still unbroken.

For the Nobility, drawing a human into their company was part of how they fed, colored as it was by their aesthetic appreciation of sucking the life from someone beautiful. But at the same time, the act was also filled with the pleasure of violating the unwilling, as well as the twisted sense of superiority that came from raising one of the lowly commoners to their own level.

Mayerling had done nothing of the sort. He did no more than lead the girl from her home, taking her by the hand as he let her into his carriage and nothing more. He had not used freedom-stealing sorceries, nor veiled threats of violence against her family to force her compliance. The girl had quietly slipped out of the house of her own accord.

From time to time, such things did happen. Bonds formed between the worlds of the humans and of the supernatural. However, they didn't necessarily become a lasting bridge between the two worlds, and typically the couple concerned would be chased by a stone-wielding mob. As was the case with these two.

The Nobility flickered in the light of extinction, and the girl had lost any world she might return to, so where could the two of them go? Out among the stars.

Mayerling raised his face.

"What is it?"

"Nothing," he replied. "It seems the dawn will be early today. If we're to gain a little more ground, I shall have to see to the horses." Kissing the girl on the cheek, he returned to the coachman's perch like a shadow.

Whip in hand, it was not to the fore that he first turned his gaze, but rather to the darkness behind them. In a place cut off from all the rest of the outside world, he heard the clomp of iron-shod hoofs approaching from far off. "So soon," he muttered to himself. "That would be D, wouldn't it?"

A crack sounded at the horses' hind as his whip fell. The scenery on either side flew by as bits and pieces. However, the ear of the Noble caught the certain fact that the hoofbeats were gradually growing closer.

"Just a little further to the river," Mayerling muttered. "Hear me, O road that lies between him and me. Just give me another ten minutes, I beseech thee."

†

"Oh. He's finally catching up," Nolt said. In the cloud that held his gaze, a small luminous point began winking ahead of D. Light spilling from the windows of the carriage, no doubt. "Give him another five minutes. No matter which one buys it, it's all sweet for us. So, what kind of vision you gonna show us next, bro?"

He didn't get to ask Borgoff anything, as his words died down to muttering when he saw how the oldest of the clan was completely focused on the mirror, to the exclusion of all else.

Perhaps it was due to this unprecedented sorcery, a magic that could choose one scene at will from the moon's gaze—which was privy to all things on earth—and then use cloudbanks as a screen for projecting that scene, but, for whatever reason, every scrap of flesh on Borgoff's colossal frame seemed to have been chiseled off. He looked half-shriveled, almost like a mummy.

When Nolt turned his eyes once again to the screen in the mass of clouds, he muttered a cry of surprise. At some point, the scenery rushing by D on either side had become desolate rocky peaks. "Well then, big bro, you thinking of maybe starting a landslide or something to bury the bastards?"

†

At last, Mayerling's darkness-piercing vision caught the black rider. The tail of his coat sliced through the wind, billowing out like ominous wings.

Could he face and beat this foe on equal terms? While he was fairly self-confident, anxiety was beginning to rear its ugly, black head in Mayerling's bosom. Though they'd only met for a split second, the force and keenness of the blade that'd assailed him from overhead lingered all too vividly in his left hand even now. The numbness was finally beginning to fade. But more than that, the distinct horror of learning the steely hand-armor that could repel laser beams had been cut halfway through rankled him, and caused him concern.

Vampire Hunter D could not be underestimated.

Mayerling's eyes glowed a brilliant crimson, and the curving black claws creaked as they grew from his right hand, which still clenched the whip.

Perhaps anticipating the new death match about to be joined, even the wind snarled. Up ahead, a wooden bridge was visible. The sound of running water could be heard. The current sounded rather strong.

Mayerling's gaze was drawn up. Quickly bending over, he pulled a pair of black cylinders from a box beside the driver's seat. They were molecular vibro-bombs, complete with timers. The molecular particles within them were subjected to powerful ultra-high speed vibrations, and they could destroy cohesive energy to reduce any substance to a fine dust.

Raising a tremendous racket, the carriage started across the bridge. The span was about sixty feet in length. Some thirty feet below, a white sash raced by. Rapids.

He halted the carriage as soon as it was across, then turned. Grabbing the molecular vibro-bomb's switch with his teeth, he gave it a twist. They weren't exactly a weapon befitting the Nobility.

D was on the bridge roughly five seconds later. He rushed ahead without a moment's hesitation.

He didn't think he was being foolish. This Hunter must've had the self-confidence and skill to deal with any situation. There was no choice, then, but for Mayerling to exert every lethal effort in return. "I had hoped to settle this like men, one on one," he muttered as he listened to the thunder of the iron-shod hoofs. "See how you like this, D—"

But the instant he jerked his arm back to prepare for the throw, lightning flashed before his eyes. It'd flashed down without warning from a black mass of clouds clogging the sky, aiming to strike the top of the bridge—and the road right in front of D.

Sparks flying without a sound dead ahead, how could the Hunter avoid the gaping ten-foot-wide hole that suddenly yawned before him? The legs of his horse clawed vainly at air, and D, keeping his graceful equestrian pose, plummeted headfirst toward the fierce, earth-shaking rapids below.

III

Just as Nolt shouted, "You did it!" Borgoff's greatly withered frame suddenly slumped forward.

On hearing the commotion, Kyle sluggishly stuck his head out, too. "What happened?" He looked out the window and up at the sky, but the screen-like properties of the clouds had been lost along with Borgoff's consciousness. "Oh, man, bro—you went and used it again, didn't you? And you're the one who's always going on about how it takes three years off your life every time you do."

Feeling the derisive jibe, the oldest brother said in a halting voice like that of the dead, "He fell into the river. Dhampirs ain't swimmers . . . Nolt, find him and finish him off."

A few minutes later, after he'd watched the second oldest depart in a cloud of dust, Borgoff gave Kyle the order to drive. He headed for the bedroom in the rear to rest his weary bones. There was one set of bunk beds on either side for his siblings. His alone was especially large, and located the furthest in the back.

As he was making his way down the aisle, trying to keep his footsteps as quiet as possible, his meatless but still sizable arm was grasped by something eerily cold. Borgoff turned around.

A white hand that could easily be mistaken for that of a genuine mummy stuck out from the bottom right bunk.

"Hey, I didn't know you were up. I'm sorry if that idiot Nolt disturbed you with all his hollering." Where the eldest Marcus normally kept this gentle tone of voice was a complete mystery.

The person in the bunk turned over, though it was clearly painful to do so. He was a pitifully small lump beneath the blankets. "I'm sorry, bro . . .about not carrying my own weight . . . "

In response to the frail voice, Borgoff shook his head without a word. His bull neck creaked and looked like it might pop. "Don't talk nonsense. The four of us are more than enough to take anyone on. You ought to keep quiet and get your rest." After he stroked it lightly, the slender hand finally pulled back into the blankets. "So," Borgoff added, "it doesn't look like you'll be having any seizures for a while then, eh?"

At this entirely sympathetic question, the other man let the covers he'd pulled up over his head slip back down smoothly. "I'll be okay," he said. "I think I'll be able to keep it under control on my own." His face was smiling as he answered feebly. His brother knew he had to be smiling, but the expression turned out to resemble nothing so much as a rictus. His cheeks were hollowed, his terribly cloudy eyes were sunken in cavernous sockets, and the breath that leaked out with his voice from lips the color of earth was as thin as that of a patient at death's door. The feeble body belonged to Grove, the infirm younger brother Nolt mentioned when the clan first met D.

However, if he were to catch a glimpse of these corpse-like features, even D himself would have been surprised. Grove's face, which held a childlike innocence, was etched with exactly the same features as the vital young man who'd slaughtered the army of attacking vampires that day in one blow, and then left.

†

M ayerling watched almost absentmindedly as his fearsome pursuer was sucked into the dirty torrent below the bridge and was lost from view in a matter of seconds. Mayerling didn't notice that the girl had opened the light-impermeable curtains and poked her head out the window.

"What happened?"

Turning around at the sound of her anxious voice, he replied, "It's nothing. Just one less thing to bother us."

Seeing the bridge behind the carriage, where flames and black smoke were still rising, the girl's face clouded quickly. "What on earth—" she gasped. "Did you make that hole?"

Mayerling wouldn't answer. He could feel in his bones that this was the work of another foe.

It wasn't lightning that'd bored a hole through the bridge, but a destructive energy-beam of another sort. Even now, a swarm of over two thousand satellites loaded with beam weaponry continued their long slumber in geostationary orbit some 22,500 miles above the Earth. Many of them had been launched by the government to help keep the human rebellion down, but there were also numerous privately owned satellites. Each of them was equipped with a means of generating beams that were decidedly man-made. What they fired was quite unlike the natural energy generated by storms. Judging from the beam's accuracy, and how it seemed to be only aiming at D, it'd been fired by a human, and one who undoubtedly felt some animosity toward D. That much was evident; any who would've wished to help Mayerling had long since perished.

It was probably another Hunter. A foe who should be feared for different reasons than D. But was it just one?

Training his boundlessly cold and dark pupils on the silver serpent of current, Mayerling presently turned to face the girl again. "Be assured . . . with the passing of but two more nights, we shall be at the gateway to the stars. Sleep well. Relax, and trust everything to me."

When the girl nodded and pulled back inside, Mayerling looked up at the moon hanging in the heavens and muttered, "Two more days . . . but daylight will come shortly. I wonder if I'll encounter this new foe before those days have passed?"

†

E ven a torrent that flowed with enough force to split rocks lost its ferocity when it had come so far, and when it hit the shore here it no longer bared its fangs. The river widened, and here and there the glimmer of silvery scales from fish leaping out to seek the light of the moon rippled along the surface of the water. Occasionally, the water ran translucent all the way down to the riverbed, and the way colossal snakelike shapes swam upstream on a zigzagging path was rather unsettling.

On the trail that ran just a little way above the riverbank, a rider muttered, "Well, this should put me right in the neighborhood now." The rider, Nolt Marcus, the oldest of the clan, halted his mount. In accordance with Borgoff's orders, Nolt had set off to find and destroy D after D had been swallowed by the muddied current. This is how far Nolt had gone.

The spot was about two miles downstream of the bridge. Along the spine of the eastern mountains, a foreshadowing of the thin blue light of dawn had come calling, but the darkness swathing the world was still thick and black.

Scanning his surroundings, Nolt reached for his hexagonal staff with his right hand. "I don't think I'll find him any farther downstream. So, did the bastard make it out without drowning then?" the Marcus brother wondered aloud. "Then again, I don't see how a dhampir could manage a stunt like that . . . "

The tinge of displeasure in Nolt's voice was due to the fact the species known as dhampir had many of the characteristics of supernatural creatures. As a blood mix between the Nobility—the vampires—and humans, dhampirs inherited some of the physical strengths and weaknesses of both. From the Nobility, dhampirs inherited the ability to recover from injuries that would be considered lethal to a human being. On the other hand, dhampirs lost up to seventy percent of their strength in daylight, they felt an unbridled lust for the blood of the living when they were hungry, and, perhaps strangest of all, not one of them could stay afloat in water.

At the beginning of the era of mankind's Great Rebellion, the vampires' utter lack of buoyancy was prized as one of the few possible ways to dispose of them. However, when it became clear that drowning itself had markedly milder results when compared to stakes or sunlight, a much dimmer view of immersion's value as a countermeasure was adopted. Drowning caused the heart to stop functioning and the body to cease all regeneration, but these effects were easily undone with the coming of night and an infusion of fresh blood.

But so long as a vampire was denied either blood or the onset of night, it would be impossible for him to recover from drowning. In other words, after an immersion, it was possible to put the comatose Nobility to the torch or to seal him away in the earth forever. Because vampires were so vulnerable after drowning, running water still served mankind in reasonably good stead.

That's what Borgoff was talking about when he told Nolt to "Finish him off."

"I'm glad you could make it."

The low voice made Nolt's whole body stiffen. Just for an instant, though. His hexagonal staff ripped through the air behind him—in the direction of the voice. It was as if his right hand had become a flash of brown. The strange thing was, the arc his weapon painted with the speed of light was a full circle. Surely enough, the hexagonal staff had grown to nearly twice its former length, stretching toward the spot from which the voice had issued.

However, when Nolt spun around dumbstruck by the lack of contact, the pole in his hands was no longer than normal.

"That's quite an unusual skill you have, sir," the youth of hair-raising beauty said in a voice of steel from atop a cyclopean block of stone that loomed by the side of the road.

No reply was given, but a flash of brown shot out. The spot it touched blasted apart, and in the midst of the scattered chips of stone D flew through the air like a mystic bird. Had his gelid gaze caught the mark the pole left on the rocky surface?

In Nolt's hands, the staff that plowed through almost diamond-hard stone like it was clay changed direction easily and raced for the airborne D.

There was a glimmer in D's right hand. The arc of brown was countered by a flash of silver, and there was a dull thud. Not giving Nolt time for a second attack, as soon as he landed right in front of the Marcus brother, D swung his blade down.

Tasting the blood-freezing fear of that blade all the while, Nolt leapt backward. The attack he unleashed as he leapt was not a swing but rather a jab, and his staff seemed to grow without end as it struck for D's face. Though he didn't seem to move a muscle, the pole missed D by a fraction of an inch as he launched himself into the air.

A flashing sideways slash. The blade that would've put a diagonal split down the middle of Nolt's face bit instead into the pole that shot up, and the two figures broke to opposite sides.

The end of his staff still aimed at D's chest, Nolt was breathing hard. Tidings of his fear. A thread-thin line of vermilion ran down the middle of his face from his forehead, and it widened at his jaw. That was the work of the blade D brought down as soon as he'd landed.

However, the blood trickling down his face wasn't Nolt's only concern. His hexagonal staff wasn't a mere piece of wood, but rather its center was packed with a steel core that, despite its thinness, could still deflect a high-intensity laser beam. Yet the pole was missing about a foot off one end. Realizing that it'd been chopped off while he was in midair, Nolt lost much of the fever in his blood.

"You son of a bitch," he growled, finally managing to say something. "So I guess you ain't no plain old dhampir, are you?"

"I'm a dhampir," D answered, still holding the same pose in his opponent's blue eyes.

Nolt's mouth twisted up in a smile. "Is that a fact? Then how do you like these apples?" With these words, his staff spun in a circle and struck the ground next to him.

With a gut-wrenching rumble, a chunk of ground a yard in diameter collapsed in on itself. This was no ordinary hollow. Maintaining a depth of about a foot, it became a ditch running all the way to the river.

About to pounce once again, D turned his eyes to this subsidence. Madness gripped the once calmly flowing water. As it coursed down the ditch from the shore, the water gathered intense speed, and, slapping up against the banks, it rose like a living creature. In great rolls, the water gushed into the space between the two of them. First the ankles and then the boots of both D and Nolt sank below the surface.

"How about it, dhampir? Can you move?" Nolt asked with a smile. It was the smirk of a victor. "You know, I've thrown down with your kind before. And this is what I did then. When a part of a dhampir gets wet, it kinda gets all stiff, don't it?"

D didn't move. Perhaps he couldn't move?

"Die, you bastard!" Nolt screamed as he charged forward. Getting a solid grip on the bottom part of the staff, he brandished it like he was going to bring it straight down and smash D's head open. The water splashed from his feet, and he kicked off the ground.

Black lightning raced up from below. Higher and faster than the staff, it danced up over his head. The last thing Nolt saw was the thick water stretching up from the ground like a tenacious predator clinging to D's black boots.

Split by D's blade from forehead to chin, by the time Nolt had fallen back to earth he wasn't breathing anymore. A bloody mist reeled out from his remains.

Without so much as a glance at Nolt as he collapsed in a heap, D walked back behind the rocks where he'd first appeared. His horse was waiting there. Coat billowing as he straddled his mount, the Hunter's eyes were eternally cold as he set them upstream, but they held a hint of sadness as well.

"Run if you like," D murmured. "But I'll still catch you."

While his words hung in the air, his horse clambered down to the shore. Without pausing, it stepped into the water. It wasn't shallow. The river would be about waist-deep on D while mounted.

If anyone was watching, they would've thought the horse was leaping across the surface of the water. Making a massive bound, the horse sank only hoof-deep before continuing to take one effortless leap after another, kicking up a little white spray as it carried D across the wide river.

There couldn't be all that many stones submerged just an inch or so below the water's surface. But clearly it was within D's power to find them in a split second and maneuver his horse onto them.

A Village of Freaks

CHAPTER 3

I

E lsewhere, another confrontation was about to unfold.

The Marcus clan's bus was approaching a section of reddish brown valley, some thirty miles from the bridge.

The reason Kyle hadn't been sent along ahead was that Borgoff had calculated the speed of the carriage and the time left until daybreak, deciding that the bus itself would be sufficient to catch up with their foe. Added to that was the fact that, if Kyle left, he would have had to look after Leila and Groveck himself. Plus, he had reservations about letting Kyle tackle the situation on his own.

He was also worried about Nolt, whom he'd sent to dispatch D. Though considering his brother's special skills with that staff, the task of finishing off a Hunter who'd almost certainly drowned should be easier than busting a baby's arm. Once they'd wrapped up their work here, they could always just shoot off a flare and call him back.

"Hold on. That's a flare," said Kyle, squinting to see it while he kept his grip on the wheel.

"What's that?" Borgoff asked, poking his rough face out of the bedroom. A single streak of light rose into a sky already bright with the radiance of dawn. The streak quickly grew several times more brilliant. "A flare way out here, smack dab in the middle of nowhere? I'd say that couldn't be nothing but the Nobility."

"*Bingo!* Roughly three miles from here. We'll be on them in five minutes. The bastard ain't gonna be able to move a muscle." Laughing confidently, Kyle added, "One good jab'll do it!" As he licked his lips, Kyle stroked the tip of one of the stakes secured to the wall.

"Still, there's something I don't like about this," Borgoff said, folding his arms. "What does he hope to gain by firing off a flare way out here? Even if he wanted help, there ain't no one who'd come . . . " After some consideration, Borgoff suddenly raised his bearded countenance again. "No fucking way!" he gasped. "We'd better make some speed, Kyle. If my hunch is right, that bastard might've called in some serious trouble."

Kyle's face grew tense at his brother's grave tone. "Here we go!" he shouted.

With a sharp change in gear and a stomp on the accelerator, the bus raced forward. The scene outside the windows started to course by at an intense speed. The scenery of the stony mountain crags grew more and more desolate. White smoke gushed from the earth in odd spots and crept heavily along the ground, evidence of nearby volcanic activity. The area around the vents was caked with yellow lumps of sulfur. Even the rocks formed extraordinary shapes—some menacing the heavens like spears, others looking so impossibly fragile that they'd crumble at a touch.

The mere passing of the vehicle caused cracks to form here and there in the depressed earth, and, when something watery but not quite the shade of blood squirted up from below, the tiny insects that flew slowly through this world were seized by spasms and dropped to the ground.

A number of times the bus plowed over bleached bones—mountains of them, contributed by everything from huge fang-baring beasts down to the smallest of vermin. The atmosphere was permeated not only by sulfur, but by strong toxins as well.

Before long, the road narrowed and the rocky surface to either side grew higher, giving the dramatic effect of an avalanche about to sweep over the bus. Neither Kyle nor Borgoff could conceal their concern.

They continued down the menacing road through the valley for about twenty minutes. Then, without warning, Kyle slowed down. "There it is!" he shouted.

Ahead of them, the blurred form of the carriage was visible in the depths of the swirling white smoke.

"What should we do, bro? Just keep going and ram 'em?" The bus had plates of armored steel bolted to the front, after all.

"Nope," the older brother replied. "Gotta keep in mind the girl might still be alive. Anyway you slice it, the Noble can't move by daylight. We'll get out and take care of 'em. Put on a gas mask."

When the two brothers had turned themselves around, the door to the bedroom opened and Leila looked out. Not surprisingly, her complexion was still pale, but her eyes blazed with the will to fight. "Picked a hell of a place to stop," she said. "Did you find them?"

"You get some rest now. And look after Grove," Borgoff said as he slipped on his gas mask.

"No way! Let me go with you!" Leila caught the oldest of the clan by the arm. The muscles felt like stone. "This is a Noble we're dealing with. Even if he can't move during the day, that still doesn't mean he'll be defenseless. You can use all the backup you can get."

"A gimp would just get in the way," Borgoff replied.

"But—"

"Leila, why don't you give it a rest?" Kyle interjected, a javelin tight in his grip. On his right hip, there hung another gas mask he intended to use for the abducted girl. "Look, you heard what Borgoff said. He told you to just leave this to the two of us. I mean, look how high the sun still is. There ain't nothing to worry about."

His voice was coaxing, but had a touch of carnal desire in it, and Leila turned away. She nodded, apparently giving in.

"Now don't you go out there!"

With that final admonishment, Borgoff and Kyle stood on the steps by the door. When Kyle pressed the switch by his side, a semitransparent veil descended from overhead, sealing the two of them off from the rest of the vehicle. This wasn't the first time they had to stalk their quarry in a poison-shrouded environ.

Opening the door manually, the two stepped down to the ground. They wore no other protection besides the gas masks. Artificial antibodies in their blood could handle the rest of the poisonous vapors and radiation.

Their feet didn't make the slightest sound as they hustled over the ground.

The Noble's carriage was motionless, just branding the earth with its faint and lonely shadow. Even the six black steeds hung their heads, appearing either to sleep or to be absorbed in contemplation.

Contrary to what one might expect, this picture of defenselessness sowed seeds of tension and anxiety in the hearts of the pair. Kyle adjusted his grip on the javelin.

Ten feet to the carriage. White smoke robbed the pair of their vision, then cleared.

Without a sound, the pair leapt to either side. Between them and the carriage there suddenly stood a black silhouette. The elongated figure garbed in a black hooded robe seemed to be an illusion, something conjured up by the poisonous vapors.

"Who the hell are you?" Kyle asked in a low voice. The filters on their masks doubled as voice amplifiers.

Giving no answer, the shadow raised its right hand. Flying with a dull growl, a steel arrow pierced it through the wrist. The shadow shook.

There hadn't been just one arrow. Thanks to Borgoff's masterful skill, arrows also stuck in the shadow's head and the left side of its chest. While it was true they were dealing with an unknown element here, three arrows may have been overdoing it a bit. But then, that was the Marcus way of doing things.

The shadow turned its face up. The brothers' eyes opened wide. The hood was empty.

When the plain robe fell flatly to the ground with three arrows still stuck in it, Borgoff forgot to launch a second attack. Something had occurred to him, and, with no warning, he turned and loosed an arrow at the carriage. As he watched it punch nicely through the polished iron plating to the rear, the vehicle's window lost its contours, the wheels twisted limply, and the entire carriage became a single sheet of black cloth trailing along the ground.

A silver flash raced off burning through the white smoke. It etched a graceful arc and ran through the horses' necks. It was the flash of a crescent blade. Their heads drooped, thick necks hacked nearly in half.

No blood came out. There was no flesh or cross section of vertebrae to be seen in the fresh wounds. The inside was hollow. The pair watched in a daze as every last one of the half-dozen horses became black cloth and settled softly on the ground.

Eerie laughter rose like smoke around them. High and low, the weird but beautiful voice that seemed to escape from the bowels of the earth was that of a woman.

About thirty feet ahead of the pair, a slender feminine figure came into focus. Laughing haughtily, she said, "Followed a Noble all this way, have we? I came out here to see the extent of your abilities, but, as I expected, they really don't amount to much. As such, naught awaits you on this road but the boiling fires of hell. You'd do well to scamper off now with your tails between your legs."

Sensing an inordinate evil in the chiming golden bell that was her voice, Kyle shouted, "You the one who pulled that hocus-pocus just now?!" The javelin was in his left hand, and his right held one of his deadly crescent blades at the ready.

"Unfortunately, no," the woman said. "Although, you're actually quite fortunate it wasn't me. Otherwise you wouldn't have gotten off with a mere prank. If you value your boring little lives, you'd best turn back posthaste."

"Where's the Noble?" inquired Borgoff. The strange thing was, he had both eyes shut tight.

"In our village," the woman replied. "He came to retain the finest guards as insurance against maggots like you following him." Laughing snidely, she added, "Perhaps you boys should hire a few of us, too, to serve as Hunters and go after him?"

Beneath his gasmask, Kyle's face grew black with rage. His left hand went into action. When the javelin flew through the air and passed vainly through the figure of the woman only to be embedded in the wall of rock behind her, indistinct shapes appeared all around them, hovering in the air. All of the shapes looked like the woman.

"Bitch," Kyle spat after the flash of crescent blade he swept around passed through the specters without meeting any resistance. He looked to his older brother. "So that's what you were up to, Borgoff?"

Eyes still shut, the giant nodded, and the sneering yet mellifluous laughter stole into their ears again.

"You still don't understand, do you, little fools? May you wander this poison smoke for all eternity." A split second later, her words became a scream.

One of the shimmering figures behind them had been pierced by Borgoff's arrow. When and how the giant fired was a mystery. Kyle hadn't seen his brother's hands move. What's more, his bow and the arrow cocked in it had been pointed straight ahead from the start.

Blood's own aroma mixed with the stench of poisonous smoke.

"You . . . you bastard!" she screeched, the shadowy figures fading as quickly as her cry.

"Bro, you did it!"

"Yep." Borgoff gave a nod, and perhaps it was the knowledge that the woman was gone for good that made his tiger-like eyes shine so strangely. Immediately, the brothers headed back toward the bus.

The door closed, and, once the poisonous gas had been evacuated through the exhaust vents, they entered the main cabin. There, for the first time, Borgoff struck the wall of the vehicle with his boulder of a fist. The ceiling rattled.

"What do you wanna do now, bro?"

"This is a huge fucking mess now. That bastard Noble's gone and holed up in the village of the Barbarois."

Kyle wasn't the only one who grew tense at his brother's words. Leila, who'd been waiting for them, reacted the same way. For the first time, something resembling paling fear flowed through the faces of the siblings. But even that was transient.

"Sounds like fun," Leila muttered, and it even seemed a vermilion flush of excitement was rising in her pale face. "The village of the Barbarois—monsters and freaks have been interbreeding there for five thousand years, honing their sorceries and skills in the darkness. I always hoped to try my hand against them someday."

"Damn straight." Kyle bared his teeth. "If he's holed up in their village, there's a pretty damned good chance he'll— well, actually, the woman already told us what he was gonna do. Said he'd come to hire her and others. There ain't no two ways about it, he's definitely got himself some freaky guards now." Kyle snickered. "I'm just itching for a piece of them. We've all heard rumors about the supernatural powers of the Barbarois. The question is, whose skills would come out on top, ours or theirs? I mean, wouldn't it be great to throw down with them just once?"

"Of course it would," the oldest Marcus replied. "I don't care if it's the Barbarois or the Nobility's Sacred Ancestor himself, we'd dye our hands in their blood. Just one thing, though. Our first order of business is that bastard Noble and the ten million dalas. I don't wanna do any fighting unless we're getting paid for it. For the time being, we'll keep a watch on this nest of freaks and wait for Nolt to get back. Me and Kyle will go. Leila, you send up a flare as soon as you're clear of this corner of hell and then wait there for Nolt."

The brutal siblings looked at each other and let out a lurid, blood-curdling laugh. What then was this village of the Barbarois that even they found so difficult to dismiss? Who resided there? And what were their darkness-spawned powers?

II

Down the road three miles from the spot where the Marcus brothers encountered the strange woman, a particularly high and rocky mountain loomed off the left-hand side of the road.

To the eye of the uninformed traveler, the heap of countless rocks, large and small, was merely a product of nature. But, upon closer inspection, the pieces of stone that at a glance had seemed to be stacked haphazardly were, in fact, arranged systematically by someone or something with an understanding of dynamics. And, as the arrangement of the rocks became clear, so too did the eerie aura surrounding them. A chill was carried down like a ghost from the icy heights of the mountain, rising up the backs of the most courageous and the most fearful travelers alike.

Though the mountain looked like it might be easily scaled, no matter how tough the human that challenged it was, partway up its scaly surface the rocks were laid out in such an intricate way that they'd cave in a second. Even if by some slim chance a climber got through that part, there were places on the route where every rock was rigged to bury the climber in an avalanche of stone.

Still, if fortune smiled on them and, by some miracle, the climber made it into the bowels of the mountain, their eyes would be greeted by a single cavern. While passing through it they'd be blasted by damp winds that seemed to blow from the very netherhells, and then they'd soon come to a fortress constructed from cyclopean stones and colossal trees. Despite the fact that the very human sounds of laughter, shouting, and crying could be heard constantly, and the smoke from cook fires never ceased, there was something in the atmosphere that separated this place from the world of humanity, an eldritch aura which hung in the air. This was the nest of demons that made the Marcus clan shudder—the village of the Barbarois.

It was a mystery just how on earth the carriage and the six-horse team drawing it had got into the village, but enter they did as the light of dawn was finally beginning to swell with the vitality of day.

There were houses in the village, and plenty of men and women. Stopping where they worked or poking their heads out of doorways, they formed a ring around the carriage the instant it came to a halt. Perhaps they were already cognizant of the true nature of their strange visitor, for not one of them tried to open the door.

Pushing his way through the ring which was now several bodies deep, an old man with a hoary mane came into view. His white beard was long enough to sweep the ground, and his back was so stooped that his chest was parallel to the earth. Untold centuries old, his face was obscured by countless wrinkles, and yet every inch of him brimmed with an ineffable vigor.

He approached the door on the left-hand side of the carriage and rapped lightly on the steel surface with his cane. Following that, he nodded to himself, and, after turning around to give a wink to the masses behind him, he put his withered, clay-like ear to the door.

The wind died out immediately.

The deathly silence persisted for what seemed like hours, but in due time the old man started to nod with the kindly countenance of a codger doting on his grandchildren.

"I see, I see. I'm glad you came. It's guards you desire then, to protect your lady love? Very well, very well. So, how many do you need? Three? Hmm, did you have anyone particular in mind?"

The eyelids he had shut like a thin line flew open. A fearsome light spilled from them, but, after a moment, he closed his eyes once more.

"Bengé, Caroline, Mashira . . . Oh, those are the very best, the cream of our village. Fine. When your flare informed us that you were being followed, Caroline headed out to toy with those wandering mongrels, but they'll be back presently. They are entirely at your disposal."

Could one of the Nobility, who should be comatose by day, be holding a conversation with this old man? Not one of those assembled seemed to find this the least bit suspect as the old man's eyes suddenly opened again.

"Oh, so you say you have one more favor to ask," the old man muttered. "What's that? There's another who follows you solo, you say? Hmm . . . a dhampir."

The air stirred violently. None of the villagers moved an inch, as if a ghastly white aura had enveloped them. Moans of shock came from the villagers' lips as the following words slipped from the old man: "His name is—D."

In a while, when silence once again ruled the scene, the mutterings of the old man were adorned with a tremble of unbridled delight. "Ah, the greatest Vampire Hunter on the Frontier—I believe we're up to the challenge. If we lure him into our stronghold and attack, slowly wearing him down, that is. That service, however, shall cost you quite dearly."

†

An hour after his brothers had gone, Groveck's condition took a strange turn. His breathing became rapid and shallow, and sweat gushed from his lean face. His state was more serious than usual, which panicked Leila. His pulse was racing, too.

"A seizure," she mumbled to herself. "But not like any we've ever seen before. What in the name of hell is this . . . "

She put as much ibuprofen as she could into the bottle on his IV, and she was headed toward the kitchen to cool down the cloth for mopping the sweat from his brow when the bus rocked violently.

Metal eating-utensils fell one after another to the floor, and though the sound-dampening carpet tried to preserve the silence, the vehicle was filled by a cacophony. Every wound in the girl's body pulsed sheer agony.

Hastily securing the IV bottle with electrical tape, Leila raced around the vehicle looking out all of the windows, checking in every direction. There was no one out there. They were parked in the middle of a circular clearing about a hundred yards in diameter that wasn't far off the road. With a click of her tongue, Leila dove into the garage to the vehicle's rear.

Ignoring the five cyborg horses stored there with their limbs retracted, she leapt into the driver's seat of her battle car. As Leila turned the key in the ignition, a comforting vibration swept through her. Without looking at the digital gauges beside the steering yoke, Leila grasped the condition of the car like it was something she could hold in her two hands.

"Atomic fuel at ninety-eight percent of capacity . . . Engine, check . . . Stabilizers, check . . . Puncture damage, negligible. Propulsion voltage good to go up to ninety-seven percent. Weapon controls, okay . . . Here we go!"

The rear doors of the bus opened, and, without waiting for the ramp to slide into place, the battle car flew out. She gave it full throttle just as it touched down and took it for a loop around the bus.

The bus was the only thing shaking, and there really was no one out there after all.

Leila parked the battle car broadside to seal off the entrance to the clearing, then stood up in her seat like a vengeful god. "Who's there? C'mon out. I'm Leila Marcus, of the Marcus clan. You won't catch me running and hiding," she declared, trying to keep the pain that knifed through her body from showing on her face. Then, as suddenly as it began, the shaking of the bus stopped.

A cheerful voice came in response. "My, missy, aren't you the high-spirited one."

Leila spun around in amazement. The perplexed expression she'd donned just before turning her head was because she didn't know where the distinct voice was issuing from.

There was no one behind her. Nor to her left, nor to right.

"Where are you?" she asked. "Where the hell are you?! C'mon out, you lousy coward!"

"There's nowhere to come out from," the voice jeered. "I'm right beside you. If you can't see me, the fault is with your eyes."

Her blood nearly curdled. Once again, she scanned her surroundings. She realized the voice spoke the truth. Whoever it was, they had to be somewhere. Right under her very nose, no less.

Leila harnessed every fiber of her being to search in all directions. Like her brothers, she'd honed her five senses to a razor-sharp level. Now her hearing and her sense of touch told her there wasn't another living creature in the clearing. Yet, despite that, she could hear the voice.

Leila was seized by a fear unlike any she'd felt before. It sprang from a loss of self-confidence and wounds that hadn't fully healed.

With the sliver gun from her side now in hand, Leila jumped out of the car. Her bloodshot eyes darted around her. She hadn't given up the fight yet.

A stabbing pain shot up her back.

Catching a hail of fire from the sliver gun she unleashed as soon as she whipped around, one of the chunks of rock hemming the clearing was reduced to dust. Fired by highly pressured oxygen, the half million, one-micron-long, .001-micron-wide needles in the gun could leave the walls of a Noble's castle as friable as unglazed pottery. But that didn't count for much against an unseen opponent.

Leila reached one hand around to her back. The stickiness she felt was blood. Clearly she'd been cut by some sort of blade, but she was powerless to do anything about it. Agony assailed her for a second time, and Leila fell to her knees. Her strength was dwindling rapidly.

The voice returned. "What's wrong, missy? Compared to the wound my colleague suffered, this is nothing. Nothing at all. It'll take a lot more than that to drive you mad, won't it?"

"Who the hell are you? Where are you?!"

"I already told you, didn't I? I'm right beside you. If you look hard enough, you should see me. *You don't see me because you think you can't.* Here, maybe this will help you understand?"

The Marcus girl gave an agonized cry. Fresh blood spilling from the back of her shredded shirt, Leila crouched down on the ground.

What kind of cold-blooded torture was this, slashing the flesh of a defenseless girl with deep cuts and shallow? Perhaps in some sick way her attacker was aroused by the sight of Leila in agony, because the voice had a ring akin to lust when it asked, "Well, how do you like that? Taste more pain, more suffering. Your brothers will be getting a taste of very same treatment from me before too long. Ha ha ha ha!"

The sneering laughter ended sharply. Leila could feel someone shaking intensely right beside her. An unearthly aura was gusting their way, coming from the entrance to the clearing.

Must be Nolt, she thought. *No, it's not.* Another disappointment lodging in her breast, Leila twisted her face around in desperation.

It was unclear how he'd gotten by the battle car, but a black-garbed youth stood casually in the center of the clearing, not making a sound. Forgetting her pain at the beauty of the one who now gazed at her, Leila swooned in glorious intoxication. The unsettling presence vanished in an instant.

Waiting for a while on horseback while he seemed to size up the situation, D quietly guided his horse to Leila's side. "Your opponent's not here any more," he said. "Can you stand?"

Torpidly, Leila pulled herself up. "No problem at all, as you can see. What in blazes brings you here?" Her bluster carried no animosity. Borgoff had told her that someone had taken care of her when she was hurt, and no one but this gorgeous young man could've fit that bill.

"I saw your flare and came. Where's the rest of your clan?"

"In the bus. Try anything funny and they'll come flying out here," Leila lied.

"So they're just sitting back watching their little sister do battle, eh? The Marcus clan has hit a new low."

At D's tone, which merely conveyed the truth without sarcasm, Leila became enraged. She staggered. The substantial blood loss she'd suffered had caught up with her. Her other wounds hadn't healed yet, either. Glancing once more at the cold beauty of the youth staring down at her from horseback, Leila passed out.

†

The next thing she knew, she was lying on a bed. Before she had time to notice her bare skin was wrapped in bandages, Leila flipped herself over and looked toward the door. A black figure was just leaving. Without a sound.

"Wait. Please, just wait a sec!" Leila herself didn't know why she called out to him so frantically.

The shadowy figure stopped.

Leila got up. She jerked the tube out of her right arm. The attached bottle of plasma rocked wildly. It was plain to see who'd gone to the trouble of setting up her transfusion.

"Go back to sleep," he told her. "You're liable to open your wounds and wake your brother."

"Never mind him," she replied. Yet, despite what she said, she peeked in on Groveck across the aisle. Confirming that his condition was stable, Leila felt relieved.

Suddenly the piercing pain returned to her body, and she let out a groan. "Don't go," she cried. "If you go, I'll die."

The young man headed for the door.

"Hold on. Don't you even care what happens to me?" Leila didn't know why she sounded so miserable as she said this. Could it be that she simply wanted him by her side? No, that thought didn't occur to her.

She was going to follow him, but her foot caught on something and she tumbled to the floor. The scream that escaped her was no fabrication.

The youth walked over calmly and picked her up.

"My back—it's killing me." That was a lie. "Carry me as far as the bed."

The young Hunter turned his back to her again.

"Wait! What was that thing? If you leave, it might come back. Please, stay with me."

The youth turned around. "I'm the competition, you know."

"You're my savior. Mine and Grove's. And if my brothers come back, I won't let them lay a finger on you."

"There's something I should tell you first," the young man continued without concern. "I cut down your brother Nolt."

Leila's eyes shot up to him. A wild rage spread through her body. It looked like she might leap at D, but instead she let her shoulders drop. "I see," she muttered numbly. "So my brother got killed . . . I think I understand why. I mean, he went up against you, right? Wait, don't go. I want you here by my side, even if it's just for a little bit longer."

Something besides her anguished cries must have stayed the stride of the icy youth. He returned to the bedroom. Leila lay down on the bed, and the young man put his back against the wall, looking down at her.

"Why did you save me, not once but twice now?" she asked.

"I had some time on my hands."

"You're not after the Noble then?"

"I've figured out where he's headed."

"Oh, you wouldn't be kind enough to share that, would you? My brothers would be overjoyed."

"Is that your sick brother in the bed over there?" the youth inquired softly. He made no attempt to look at Groveck.

"Yep. Fact is, he hasn't even been able to walk or anything since the day he was born."

"But it seems he can do something else instead."

A look of astonishment raced across Leila face. Soon, her sober expression returned, and she said, "You're a strange one, aren't you? Saving the competition twice and all. Even though you had no qualms about killing one of my brothers. What, are you afraid taking down a woman would bring shame on your sword?"

"If you come at me, I'll cut you down."

At D's impassive words, Leila grew pale. She knew he was serious. Here was a young man with the keenness of a mystic blade concealed behind his beauty. And yet, while their eyes were locked, she wouldn't mind being slashed so long as it was D who did it. The thought that she'd even want him to kill her welled up in her breast like an enchanted fog, turning the contents of her heart and mind into slush. That must've been the power of a dhampir—the power of one descended from the Nobility.

"You're a strange guy," Leila said again. "You aren't even gonna ask me where my brothers went? If I hadn't woken up, you'd have left, wouldn't you? Like a shadow. Like the wind. Are all dhampirs like that?"

"How long have you been a Hunter?"

Her own question unexpectedly brushed aside, Leila became a bit disoriented. "How long? For as long as I can remember. Besides, I can't live any other way."

"This isn't a job for women. When it gets to the point you enjoy stalking your prey, that's proof that you're not a woman anymore."

"How tactful of you to say so. Keep your opinions to yourself," Leila said, turning away. Any other man would've had the palm of her hand or a knife headed their way. But because the youth spoke in that unconcerned tone of his—neither reproachful nor teasing—there was something in his words that shook Leila. "I can't very well change my way of life at this stage of the game," she continued. "I've got too much blood on my hands."

"It comes off if you wash them."

"Why would you say something like that? You trying to put me out of work?"

The young man made his way to the door. "The next time you see me," he said, "you'd better forget the small talk and just start shooting. I won't hold back either."

"That's just fine by me," she replied. There was a grieving hue in Leila's eyes.

"Your brothers wouldn't make much of a stink over losing one little sister," the shadowy figure said as it faded into the sunlight. "Any girl who cries out for her mother as she lays dying isn't cut out for Hunting."

And then the youth was gone. Like a shadow melting in the sun.

After he left, his words continued to ring in Leila's ears.

The girl's eyes bored into the closed door, and something in them blurred softly. Just as she was going for the door, a thin hand caught hold of her sleeve.

"Grove?!"

"Leila . . . you're not gonna listen . . . to what that guy said, are you?" The voice from under the blankets sounded furtive and twitching. "You wouldn't listen to that guy . . .go off and leave me and the others . . . now would you, Leila? Don't you forget about . . . *you-know-what* . . . "

"Quit it!"

The scrawny hand Leila tried to shake off held her entirely too tenaciously.

"Don't you ever forget that, Leila," Groveck rasped. "You belong to all of us . . . "

III

T he shadowy figures of Kyle and Borgoff clung like geckos to the rocky face overlooking the village of the Barbarois. The mountain, which was insurmountable to the average traveler, hadn't served as much of a deterrent against this pair.

Sprawled on a flat rock and inspecting the village through electronic binoculars, Kyle raised his head and said to Borgoff, "Damn it, the carriage and whatever's in it went into the forest, but they ain't come out. You think maybe they've already slipped back out the same way they got in?"

"Don't know." Borgoff shook his head. "And it's not like we can just waltz up and ask them, now can we?"

Kyle fell into silence. Somehow they'd managed to climb partway up the mountain without being detected, but even this pair of crafty devils were hesitant to sneak into the village. In fact, their Hunter instincts told them it'd be dangerous to get any closer in broad daylight.

Even though Barbarois seemed like a run-of-the-mill hidden village, with no sign of watchtowers or lookouts, the fact was that in the nondescript shade of the rocks and groves there lurked those with sight as keen as swords.

Conversing only with their eyes, the brothers decided to sneak in by night, when the watch would slacken.

The Marcus brothers knew that the Noble who owned the carriage had called on this village hoping to retain some guards. If possible, the brothers wanted to finish him before he could do so, but, now that it'd gone this far, that was no longer an option. The two brothers weren't at all confident they could slip into this mob of freaks—who were their equals or perhaps even their superiors in battle—and accomplish their aims.

Under the circumstances, there was no choice but to wait for the carriage to come out, but they had misgivings about that, too. They couldn't imagine how the carriage had possibly been brought into the village, and the prospects of it slipping out unseen were extremely good. They wouldn't know it had left until it was gone.

If only they knew the Noble's destination they could at least head him off, but they didn't even know their prey's name. *At the rate things are going, we'll never land that bounty*—the Marcus brothers grew impatient at that thought. And as they fumed, more of their precious time slipped by.

When they'd first got up to their lookout, the carriage was being moved from the square into a stand of trees. Even after they watched the people disperse from the area, it seemed there'd been some sort of a discussion. Common sense dictated that the Nobility slept by day, but then common sense didn't seem to have much say about matters in this village.

So what had they discussed? Well, the Marcus brothers actually had a pretty good idea what'd been covered. They could guess how many guards the Noble had employed and what kind they would be, and maybe where they were headed, too.

The sun was nearing noon. The rocky surface went from warm to searing, and yet the brothers still lacked a good plan. A hue of impatience was just beginning to show on Borgoff's face when he heard a sudden cry.

"Bro, is that who I think it is?!"

Checking Kyle's surprised outburst with his firm, silent gaze, Borgoff felt the same shock as his brother. Off to their left, a figure had just leisurely slipped into the black cavern leading to the village—and it looked like it was D!

"That bastard should've drowned! What, ain't he a dhampir?"

Borgoff didn't answer Kyle's question. He was having enough trouble believing it himself. "Then, I reckon that means . . . Nolt's had it."

Turning to his older brother for only a second, Kyle's face was instantly colored by hatred. "That bastard . . . Killing off Nolt . . . He's not getting out of this alive," he growled. "Ain't that right, bro?"

Though he nodded, Borgoff kept his silence. Difficult as it might be to accept, Borgoff knew that Nolt had to be dead and that D must have killed him. But killing a Noble with an escort of Barbarois would entail risking their lives. This young dhampir possessed an unearthly intensity even they couldn't match, and making an enemy of him as well would be utter madness.

"I bet that bastard's here to scope out the village, same as us. This is our chance. I'll take him down from here with my crescent blades."

As the younger brother was about to stand, Borgoff's hand took a firm grip on his elbow. "Hold your horses, okay? Look, he's headed straight for the gate. He ain't staking it out. He plans on parleying with them directly."

"You're kidding me! Dammit, ain't that even worse? If this keeps up, he's gonna beat us to the punch!"

The words of the wild youngest brother held some truth.

As Borgoff glared fixedly into space, his face grew more and more sad, and sweat started to blur his brow. When his eyes opened, there was a ghastly hue to them. "We got no choice then. I didn't wanna do this, but we'll have to call on Grove," he said.

"Wait just a minute there . . . " Kyle said, his voice rigid. This was the same brother who'd earned a glare from Borgoff for suggesting they send Groveck to scout around the village of the dead they had entered two days earlier.

What kind of power lay in that shriveled mummy of a youth that could offer a solution to their problems?

"I'll keep watch here, Kyle. Once you've given Grove a seizure, you come right back," the older Marcus said.

"Good enough."

Why was it that a lewd smile arose on Kyle's face as he answered? Whatever the reason, it only lasted an instant. Flipping himself over atop the rock, his leather garments sparkled blackly in the gleaming sunlight and he came down the mountain with the light gait of a super-natural beast. Down he went, over extremely dangerous rocks—not one of which could be tread upon without setting off an avalanche.

†

Coming within fifteen feet of the eerie gates, which looked to be wood and stone wired together and strung with hides, D halted his steed. As he looked up at the towering palisade ahead, his expression was redolent of a dashing young poet or philosopher.

The air swished to life.

Where on earth they'd been hiding was a mystery. No one could be seen or even sensed a moment earlier, but all of a sudden a number of people appeared among the rocks and trees. They surrounded D. The face of each was darkly intrepid, but some among them were pale to the point of transparency, or armored in ghastly scales. They were a band that would no doubt cow any traveler encountering them for the first time, yet, for some reason, with D they kept their distance. Once they had him surrounded, they made no move to approach him. On realizing that it was fear and wonder that arose on their inhuman faces, the Prince of Hell himself might've doubted his own eyes.

With a sharp glance from D, they staggered backward.

"I'm the Vampire Hunter D. I have business here. Kindly open the gates."

At his bidding, the mysterious gates swung silently inward. Without another glance at the guards to his fore and rear, his left and his right, D rode leisurely in on his horse.

As soon as they were inside, a terrible aura enveloped D and his steed. Triggered by the eerie emanations D himself radiated, all the eldritch energies in the air seemed to shoot toward them as one. D's expression didn't change in the least, and his horse never altered its stride.

When they had gone a few steps, the strange roiling energies disappeared. The men, who remained positioned around D, exchanged startled looks. The Hunter's unearthly aura had just beaten down their own disturbing emanations.

The village and its inhabitants flowed past D as he rode. The village had been established in a vast wooded region that'd sprung up in the middle of the mountains, and the homes were fashioned from timbers and stone. Most of the residents were self-sufficient as far as food and weapons went, and a building that looked to be a factory could be spied tucked silently among the trees.

While they were rather antiquated, there were high-caliber laser-cannons and ultrasonic wave-cannons visible within the palisade, indicating that the Barbarois were perfectly prepared to deal with their enemies in the outside world.

But what was truly astonishing was the appearance of the inhabitants of the village. Their clothing was the ordinary farm wear or work clothes found in any hamlet, but very few of the arms and legs and heads that protruded from said raiment had the form of anything human. A glimpse of red tongue could be seen flickering from what must've been lips on a face scaled like a serpent's, while another visage was mantled in thick fur like a veritable wolf. Way in the back, an innocent young boy splashed water up from his pool. From the neck down he had the body of a crocodile, and the limbs to match.

There existed things in this world that weren't entirely natural, the offspring of couplings between fiendish beasts and human beings. All who dwelled in the village of the Barbarois were the fruit of those abominable relations.

Most humans from the world below would've fainted dead away at the sight of these demons, but D rode past them silently, arriving at what seemed to be a central square. At the center stood the black carriage, along with a hoary-maned old man.

Halting his horse at the entrance to the square, D stepped to the ground.

"Oh," the old man exclaimed, stroking that ground-sweeping white beard of his. "You dismount? I see you know enough to show respect for your elders. But you have me sorely puzzled. How did you ever manage to climb our mountain on horseback?"

Whether the words that seemed to slither along the ground reached him or not, D took hold of the reins and started walking towards the old man. He stopped six feet shy of him and gestured to the black carriage with his right hand. "I'd like you to hand over the two passengers in that carriage," he said.

The old man smiled broadly—or rather, all the wrinkles on his face twisted up into a smile—but in the laughter that followed there was a hint of scorn. "Young man, you've come into our village in a way no one else has ever managed. I wish I could tell you the passengers in that carriage were yours, but it's too late, too late. We've already sided with the carriage, you see. The contract is drawn, and we've been paid in gold. Paid with the fabled ten thousand-dala coins—ten of them. Could you afford that much?"

"If I could, would you sell out your clients?"

At D's reply, soft as ever, the smile instantly vanished from the old man's face. His wrathful mien was a sight to behold, and it looked like he might even take a swing at the Hunter with his cane. But he unexpectedly threw his head back in a way that almost seemed to straighten his spine, and he gave a hearty laugh. "Ho ho ho. Knowing as you do that this is the village of the Barbarois, that took nerve to say. Oh, what a treat, what a great treat! Why, the last time anyone spoke to me like that was precisely three hundred and twenty years ago . . . "

A strange expression skimmed across the old man's face. As if groping in the misty depths of forgotten memory with fingers that'd lost their sense of touch, he narrowed his eyes impatiently. When he threw them open again, a hue of astonishment spilled from his pupils.

"That face," he murmured. "Could it be that you're . . . "

"I'm a Vampire Hunter," D said quietly. "At the request of the father of an abducted girl, I'm in pursuit of the culprit. I've come here as a result of that, and nothing more. But I understand your position. All I ask it that you put him back outside and let me pursue him in peace."

"Oh. Better yet, a man of principle." The old man seemed beside himself with joy, striking his cane against the earth. "Out of respect for that, I'll share a little something with you. What his requests were. One was that we provide him with an escort to protect him from you and other Hunters. The other was to dispose of a young man named D who was certain to come here."

The square was buried in an avalanche of killing lust. While the two were conversing, countless villagers had encircled them. Not a single one of them had a weapon in hand. Nonetheless, each and every one of them had a fearsome air that made it clear they'd have no problem slaying a few humans at a time.

"What will you do now, D? It was remarkable how you made it all the way in here, but getting back out looks to be somewhat more difficult, doesn't it? Every man and woman assembled here's been trained in the most astounding of abilities. No matter how great of a Hunter you may be, you can't possibly kill them all."

And what was D doing as the old man spoke the indisputable truth? He was looking up at the sky. Gazing at the perfectly clear blue and the clouds cavorting there.

His expression was so intent the villagers stopped closing on him and exchanged looks with each other.

"So, is that where he wants to go then?"

Perhaps mistaking the Hunter's muttering as a plea for his life, one of the Barbarois leapt into the air with a cry like a savage roc. When he straightened up, his body was round overall, yet his stomach was flat as a board, a shape that was reminiscent of a tortoise. The beast stretched his arms toward D's face. The fingertips fused with the nails and became like the horns of a bull. If they but touched him, they'd gouge away a chunk of flesh and bone.

The two figures passed each other—one in the air and one on the ground—and the rotund man landed lightly as he came back to earth.

Maybe it was the stirring of the villagers that called forth the bloody mist. A number of them had caught the silvery flash that shot out faster than the eye could follow in the instant the man had passed D. But, no—they'd certainly seen the man's head pull into his clothing just as D's blade was about to strike. Like a tortoise, the man's body was covered by a carapace that was impervious to even bullets, and his hands and feet could stretch like springs.

But his carapace cracked down the middle just as he landed. The face of the man that appeared from the bottom, the serpentine neck, the tangle of intestines—all of them had been split in two right down to the crotch, and the man sent up a spray of blood as he toppled.

For the first time, the others saw the blade shining in D's right hand. There was no one foolish enough among them to press the Hunter a second time, despite the gut-deep rage they felt at the death of their comrade and friend. The realization that this youth possessed an unholy prowess with the sword seeped into the marrow of their bones.

In an attitude and pose no different from the one that'd greeted his attacker, D turned to the old man and said softly, "You can kill me if you like, but many of your villagers will die, too. Why don't you stand back and let me stay here until night? When the carriage leaves, I'll go right out after it. That's it. As the lot of you have entered a contract to help the fugitive, I'll ask nothing else."

If the decree of certain death the old man had pronounced on D was valid, what D said was equally true.

"So, it's just as I thought then . . . " The old man nodded, his face showing understanding. "Such abilities, such dignity," he muttered. "Yes, I was right all along . . . " Then, waving his right hand so the villagers backed off, he said something unexpected in a weary tone. "If you should ask that all in the village drown in a lake of blood, I could not deny you. I implore you, take the shriveled head of this old fool for our rudeness and grant us your forgiveness."

"What are you talking about?!" someone shouted. This one angry outburst parted the wall of villagers.

A woman in a dress an unsettlingly deep shade of indigo stepped from the mob to stand between the old man and D. The spot of pink on her exposed right shoulder was strangely conspicuous against her white skin. Her voice was a venom-dripping howl as she said, "Why the fainthearted drivel? Elder, have you forgotten the law of our village? Once we have a contract with one who's come seeking our aid—regardless of who they may be— we must uphold the wishes of our employer or die trying. And I, Caroline, intend to do so, with the aid of Mashira and Bengé."

"Absolutely," an impudent voice added in agreement. Pushing his way through the ring of people, a middle-aged man of average height and medium build tossed the hem of his gray coat and took his place alongside the woman. "By failing to honor a contract we've already agreed to, you'd be doing more than just breaking the law of the village. It would mean the ruin of the village itself. Elder, leave this young pup to the three of us."

"My sentiments exactly."

The third speaker drew a dramatic reaction. The voice came from behind the middle-aged man, and it must've caught him off guard, because he flinched momentarily and took a step back.

Framed by the other two but standing behind them was a strangely elongated man, as thin as a preying mantis. His hands and face were as black as if they'd been dipped in ink, and his coat was the color of midnight. Though this was the same color as the leather Kyle garbed himself in, there was something peculiar about it that gave it an entirely different feel.

"I believe we met earlier," the tenebrous man said, winking at D. The man was so thin it seemed plausible no one would be able to see him hiding behind a fair-sized pole. But there hadn't even been a single tree nearby to conceal him. "Allow me to do the introductions. The lovely lady you see here is Caroline, while this is Mashira. And I am Bengé," he said, turning with a smile to the elder. "Since he's already here there's not much we can do. Elder, you may relent, but we're going through with this. You can strip us of our right to reside here if you so desire."

"Friends of his marred my skin," Caroline said in a quivering voice as she pressed her left hand to the pink spot. "I won't forget that. I'll never forget the pain. Even pounding an iron wedge through this rascal's chest won't make it go away!"

"There must be others besides us who feel the same way. Step forward!"

But when the middle-aged man—Mashira—had made this call, the old man shouted "Idiots!" so loudly that the rebellious trio and a number of villagers coming forward to join them flinched. That wizened feline form of the old man had caused the group of malcontents three times his size to tremble.

"Do you fools know I've looked like this since the village was founded? Have you any idea how your ancestors suffered and sweated to build this mountain village after they were chased from their homes for carnal relations with demons? I'll have you know, all their hard work was poised for destruction at one time."

Even the young ones—those for whom the past did not yet exist—were riveted in place by the purposefulness of the old man's voice. It was the sort of voice that would steal into their ears even if they had their hands clamped over them. Perhaps the only one who could ignore it was D, standing solitary and forlorn.

The bloody screams of the old man continued. "On that day—the first day of our ten-thousand-year history—a horrible toxic gas gushed from the earth and onto our land. Half the villagers died, and the other half could do naught but wait for death as their flesh festered. If a certain personage hadn't appeared, the village would've become the domain of the Grim Reaper, and none of you would've ever been born. Listen well, for that person traveled with a certain grand purpose in mind. He'd heard rumors of us, and was the first to rush here. And this is what he said. 'Let five of your strongest, bravest men accompany me on my journey. If you do, I will take away this calamity that has befallen your village, and fortune shall instantly smile upon you.'"

This was the first time more than half of the villagers had heard these facts. Engrossed by this sudden tale of days gone by, the villagers failed to notice two things that were happening. The first was that, perhaps due to something in the old man's story, D's eyes had begun to give off a piercing light. And the other was that a young man was walking down the road from the supposedly locked main gate, making his way through the deserted village as he headed towards the square.

"This entire square," the Elder continued, "and the whole village, for that matter, was filled with rotting, dying souls. But the instant that person's proposition reached their ears, they forgot all about the excruciating pain. And then, one villager came from behind a pile of rubble over there, and another came from back beyond the withered trees. The people went to him as if they'd been summoned by name—exactly five of them. What's more, they were the toughest we had, and everyone knew it."

The young man approached the entrance to the square. Taking a quick peek around, a charming smile nudged his ruddy cheeks as he headed in.

"And then, the village of the Barbarois came back to life." The old man's voice was boundlessly deep. "As soon as that personage had left with the five, why, the ground the village sits on rose toward the sky and came to be where you see it now. In the space of three breaths, new growth budded on the trees, and the flowers bore fruit. It wasn't until later we discovered the toxic subterranean gases had been diluted to harmless levels, too. All we could do at the time was chant out his name and press our faces to the ground. Heed my words!" the old man said, his voice that of the Elder that commanded all. "I'll tell you a law that you youngsters don't know about. When that person or any of his bloodline should appear, then and only then must all in the village bend any subsequent laws and comply with his wishes."

His awe-inspiring tone was an order. Even the rebellious trio was speechless.

The old man bowed deeply to the beautiful Hunter, whose black hair was swaying in the breeze. "Long have we awaited you. All that your highness desires shall be granted. If you wish that carriage ripped apart, or burnt to the ground where it stands, we are yours to command."

As they watched him with eyes full of an awe that surpassed fear, D's reply came to the villagers' ears.

"I appreciate the offer, but you have the wrong person. Let those three go and guard the carriage, as they wish. I'll be right behind them."

"What are you trying to say?" the old man asked in astonishment.

"What an honest fellow," black Bengé laughed shrilly. "Well, since he says so himself, this law you've brought up doesn't apply, Elder. But in light of his frankness, we won't let anyone else touch him. The three of us alone will take him on."

"I have one juicy tidbit for you to take to your grave," Caroline laughed, her crimson lips curling back. "This carriage is bound for the Claybourne States."

"Let's go, whippersnapper!" Mashira cried out as he crouched down. A heavy ax glittered in his right hand.

It looked like even the old man lacked the means to forestall the vicious attack by the trio. Just then, a harsh query of "Who the hell are you?!" could be heard from the rear of the crowd, but the question soon became a drawn-out scream.

The rows of people kicked up sand as they parted, and, at the far end of the straight path they opened, a rosy-cheeked young man smiled brightly. It was an angelic smile, the kind anyone would return without thinking twice. However, the fetid stench billowing up before him was part of the smoke rising from the chest of a fallen villager. Though it was unclear just what sort of energy had struck the villager, flames were still licking the carbonized and perfectly circular wounds on his chest and back.

D became a black shooting star flying through the air. The ray beam that shot through the space he'd occupied an instant earlier continued past him. With nothing to strike, it scored a direct hit to the carriage parked to one side of the square.

"That's not good!" someone cried out. Startled by the flying sparks and energy discharge, the team of horses whinnied especially loudly and bolted for the exit on the far side of the square.

"Close the back gate!"

A few villagers ran off in response to the old man's shouts, but an instant later a beam intercepted them, and they fell forward with their heads blown off. Nobody could tell where the beams were coming from. The square had become a place where bolts of light flitted madly, and, as fleeing villagers vanished in the flashes, the origin of the murderous beams still seemed impossible to determine.

However, the one clear image that greeted anyone who looked back was the enraptured expression of the angelic young man as he stood by the entrance to the square watching the mad dance of the lights. It was inspiring how his face brimmed with joie de vivre as he gleefully toyed with the deadly rays.

All at once, the square reclaimed its original hue. Perhaps it was an aftereffect of the powerful white flashes, but the green trees and brown houses burned themselves into the scene in almost painfully deep tones before gradually returning to their natural colors.

Villagers creeping to the edge of the square—or in some cases crouched on the ground watching where this supernatural phenomenon was headed—saw a pair of figures square off with some thirty feet between them. One was a young man wearing an angelic smile, the other was a Hunter as beautiful as the moon's corona.

Which would prove faster, the racing figure in black or the coursing stream of white light?

Everyone gasped as D fended off one white-hot attack but had two more streaks pierce his body as he dashed forward. But what did the villagers really see and gasp about?

D had held his left hand out in front on his chest. The two bolts of light changed direction right before him, became a single flash, and were sucked into the palm of his hand.

The young man didn't move. His smile still brimmed with pleasure.

D's flashing blade flowed from the tip of his foe's head down to his lower jaw. There was no resistance. Still holding the pose from his downward stroke, D stood a little closer to the edge of the square.

The young man had suddenly disappeared. Dim shadows that played across D's face testified this wasn't the result of anything he'd done.

The old man ran over to him. "D—Are you injured, milord?"

Without answering, D looked back across the square. There was no sign of the carriage. "Can I get down the back side of the mountain?" he asked.

The old man nodded. "There's a passage known only to the villagers. Damn!" the old man shouted, looking around desperately.

D knew why the Elder cursed. The three toughs Mayerling had retained were nowhere to be seen.

†

Kyle pulled his hot lips away from the woman's body now that resistance had given way to moaning, as it always did. From a bunk that until now had been deathly silent, there trickled the sound of shallow but urgent breathing.

"Dammit—he's back pretty damn fast this time," Kyle spat irritably and stood up. "Hey, hurry up and get that IV ready," he ordered Leila, who was still stark naked.

Glaring sharply at her older brother, the tracks of tears still fresh on her face, Leila gathered her discarded clothing.

Glancing at the bruises on her skin and the purple teeth-marks from where he'd just bitten her, Kyle clucked his tongue remonstratively. "You should've just behaved like usual and done what I told you. I don't know what got into you today, but that's what you get for being dumb and putting up a fight." Chuckling, he added, "Of course, I suppose it just made it that much easier to get ol' Grove worked up."

"Quit it!" Leila slapped away the hand reaching for her ample bosom. "Lately, the gap between his normal attacks has gotten pretty slim, you know. If you keep forcing Grove to have more on top of those, even though you know it's shortening his life, what do you think is gonna happen? If his energy goes wild, no one has any idea how bad the destruction would be."

"Shit, you think we can read that far ahead? We've got problems right now. We'll know how things went just as soon as Borgoff gets back. Nah, on second thought I think I'll try asking Grove first. Outta my way."

Cruelly pushing Leila aside, Kyle went to the pillow of the third Marcus brother.

"Hey, bro, it's me—Kyle. Tell me what you saw while you were . . . *in there*. Remember what I asked you to look into before you went?"

For quite a while the rasping sounds that escape from a patient at death's door continued, then ceased.

A sudden gasp. It hadn't come from the man beneath the blankets. A pale thin hand was wrapped around Kyle's windpipe.

"Want to know, Kyle? You want to know?" Groveck wheezed. "You're here having all the fun with Leila . . . while you put me through the tortures of hell . . . And you want to know?"

"Er . . . yeah. Sure, I wanna know." It was all the younger Marcus brother could do to answer, with the hand at his throat.

The hand quickly fell away. Groveck's delicate voice practically sobbed, "Our prey is heading for . . . the Claybourne States . . . "

The Killing Game

CHAPTER 4

I

Twilight had begun to swaddle the woods at a fork in the gently snaking road.

Gently, the girl switched off an electric light patterned after an old-fashioned candelabra. Blue darkness flooded the interior. The day that was hers alone was ending, and the world that was both of theirs was beginning.

The girl liked the sound of the lid opening on the black coffin that lay in one corner of the vehicle. Before long, his hand appeared and pushed the lid away. He stood up and stretched once, as was his habit. And then, pulling a small chair over, he seated himself in front of the girl.

Thank you. That's what he said. In appreciation of the fact she'd switched off the lights. He would never think of telling her she should've kept them on. *Thank you.* That was all.

The couple's romance had begun in the woods in spring. The traveler's carriage had struck the girl when she dashed out suddenly in pursuit of a bird, and the lone occupant had tended her wounds—hardly a unique story, but because the principal characters were a human and a Noble, it could only end in misery.

Sometimes, however, there were exceptions. The girl knew she was dealing with a Noble. And the Noble knew he was dealing with

VAMPIRE HUNTER D · DEMON DEATHCHASE | 99

a human. Yet there was neither fear nor scorn between them. They simply fascinated each other.

Their walk through the woods was sweet. For once in her life, the girl didn't fear the darkness. He'd been good enough to teach her. He'd shown her that the night, too, teemed with life.

The girl heard the flowing of a river. She saw the moonbeam fish leaping against the lunar disc. She smelled the perfume of night-blooming jasmine. She heard the poetry the wind recited, and a chorus of tiny, unseen frogs. The night was full of light, too— and he was unfailingly by her side.

He felt as she did. A heretic among the Nobility, he was one who didn't consider humanity inferior. A baron who loved the day as well, but awaited his kind's demise without ever having seen the light of the sun. Finally, he'd seen a goal, an end to his aimless wandering. The girl had given him that.

His travels had left a bitter taste in his mouth. Fleeing from villagers and Hunters hell-bent on killing Nobles, he'd crossed a brutally cold glacier. He'd raced through mountain trails whipped by howling, mad winds. All of which would've been fine if his journey had been for some purpose. Though on the road to extinction, his own destruction still lay a long way off.

And then he'd met the girl. A young lady flitting about a forest filled with living things, soaking up the light of midday. What did rank matter? So what if they were different species? They both knew who was important to them. That was all there was to it.

This chance meeting of day and night began with a gentle gaze and the bashful, tender joining of hands. The girl had just turned seventeen. He understood the hopes and fears in her heart. That being the case, couldn't a Noble and a human possibly stay together? No, not in this world.

It was then he'd broached the subject. *Would you go away with me?*

The girl nodded. *I'll go anywhere. As long as I'm with you.*

And then the two exchanged their first kiss. Devoid of lust for blood or the fear of being fed upon, it was a feverish kiss, but also a demure one.

Tragedy struck the following night. He burst into her home, unable to watch the beating the girl's father gave her when he learned his daughter was going to run away. For the first time, this Noble, propelled by hatred, sucked a human's blood. However, he failed to notice the father had a rare sort of constitution that reacted strangely to vampire attacks.

Whether a bitten human became a bloodthirsty creature like the Nobility or was left a mere mummy depended on the intent of the Noble that drained his or her blood. Though exceedingly rare, there were also some cases where what happened to the victim ran counter to the wishes of the vampire. A drained individual might be left as a human incredibly low on blood, refusing to change. And an emaciated man left to die of blood loss could come back as a vampire.

Everyone the girl's father fed on had become the same sort of fiend with a single bite. Those he attacked sought new victims, and, in the course of a single night, the whole village was transformed into pseudo-Nobility. But the girl had been rendered unconscious by the intense beating she'd received. She had seen none of this.

When she awoke, her love's gaze greeted her. And that's how their journey began. Their journey to the Claybourne States.

†

"I accomplished what I wanted to in the village, but it seems they couldn't dispose of him," the Noble muttered as he reviewed the events of the day from recordings made by the electronic eyes. "Most likely this other man with the strange powers has also learned our destination. Given the speed of this carriage, it's entirely conceivable they'll be lying in wait for us. We shall have to take the initiative."

As the girl turned her questioning eyes on him, he informed her they'd be at their destination before long. He left the vehicle. The pair of escorts riding alongside the carriage bowed to him. One was on horseback, and the other—a woman—was in a small, single-passenger buggy.

"Greetings," the first guard said. "I'm Mashira."

"And I am Caroline. I've looked forward to your appearance, Sire."

"We seem to be one short," Mayerling noted, his tone and bearing in keeping with his Noble rank.

Mashira nodded. "Yes. He's lying in wait for the enemy in the woods up ahead."

"For the enemy?" the Nobleman asked. "Alone?"

"That's correct, sir."

"There's no need to fear," Caroline said in a mysterious tone. Though Mayerling knew nothing of it, the shoulder left bare by her indigo dress no longer showed even a trace of a wound. Her gaze clinging to him as she climbed over to the coachman's perch of the carriage, she looked up at her employer and said, "He won't do anything. He's simply gone to get a peek at the other Hunters you mentioned to the Elder."

"The other Hunters?" Mayerling's beautiful countenance became a grimace, and he stated, "I'm well aware of the abilities of any other Vampire Hunters besides *him*. No, strike that—is the young man who ran amuck in your village one of them, too?"

"Most likely," Mashira replied.

Caroline added, "That woman in the car you mentioned is one as well, sire. And there may well be others. So to Bengé goes the honor of the first encounter . . . "

Mayerling was silent. From his recordings, he'd learned about the girl who'd attacked them while they were resting at the Shelter and her battle with the automated defenses. He was quite sure she'd been gravely wounded back at the Shelter, but if she was still alive then she'd prove a troublesome adversary. Even more so if she were in league with that young man from the village square . . .

"Well," the Nobleman said to the pair, "while he may be one of your fellow Barbarois, I know only his reputation, not what powers he possesses. No matter how great his abilities, it'll be no mean feat to dispose of all the enemies on my tail. Especially all alone . . . "

His two bodyguards looked at each other. Mayerling may not have realized they were smiling.

"Well, we'll be arriving in the village of Barnabas shortly," said Caroline. "Once he's returned there, perhaps you'd care to ask him about it yourself. But this alone I can tell you. If someone's already encountered him—or worse yet, is pursuing him—without a doubt they shall die before this night is through." Her words were backed with such confidence that even Mayerling, Noble that he was, was perplexed for a moment. "But all that aside, will you not do us the honor of introducing the guest you have inside? Come what may, it could prove somewhat troublesome if we don't know what she looks like."

"Absolutely," Mashira said, nodding his agreement.

After a bit of consideration, Mayerling bent over and rapped lightly on the door. "Kindly show yourself," he said.

While it was unclear how she'd heard him inside over the roar of the speeding carriage, the blue windowpane opened and a gorgeous countenance emerged. Her face was tinged with trepidation from the darkness.

"Oh, my," Mashira blurted out, and his words were not altogether empty flattery.

"Such a beauty," Caroline added, but her burning gaze was concentrated on the person in the driver's seat.

"Thank you, my love," Mayerling said, and the window closed.

At that moment, in a tiny voice even his Noble senses couldn't detect, someone tittered, mumbling, "Nice and pretty, just how I like 'em. Think I'll make her mine . . . " It was clearly the voice of a fourth person, someone who could not be accounted for.

†

The clear weather of that afternoon had broken, and leaden clouds pervaded the night sky.

A figure garbed in black sped down the street the carriage and its escorts had taken a scant hour earlier. There was no moon, but the black-garbed figure was so beautiful he virtually gave off a light of his own. With the speed with which he galloped, he could gobble up that one hour lead in less than twenty minutes if all went smoothly. Just as he was hitting the heart of the forest, however, he stopped sharply.

Though there were clouds, the darkness wasn't complete. In D's eyes, it was just like midday. About thirty feet ahead of where D halted his horse, a gigantic tree branch hung over the road, and one part of it in particular protruded sharply. Beneath that protrusion hung a long, thin shadow. D alone saw it for what it truly was. One of the trio of escorts—Bengé.

According to what Mashira had told Mayerling a short while earlier, their compatriot had come here to meet D. And, given the work each had undertaken, an encounter with the Hunter would mean a battle to the death. Bengé had already seen D in action, from the skirmish in the village of the Barbarois and the way D protected Leila in the clearing, and he must've been aware of how powerful D really was. The fact that Bengé appeared to confront D despite all that he knew indicated that he had the utmost confidence in his fighting abilities.

"Hello there," Bengé called out, his slim hand raised in a cheerful greeting, but his eyes weren't laughing. "I regret to inform you that you can't pass this way. Oh, but this is the only road to take. Then it looks like one of us will just have to wait by the side of the road—as a corpse!"

Bengé probably figured his conceited tone would draw some sort of reaction. But he let out a shout of fright as he caught sight of D flying off his horse and up over his head with lightning speed.

Indeed, talk was futile. D's sword, which never returned to its sheath without first tasting the blood of its foes, split Bengé's skull in two before he could flee. The reason D promptly spun himself around upon landing back on the ground was because of the lack of resistance his blade had conveyed. There was no sign of the clearly bisected Bengé, only a sheet of black cloth that fell about the Hunter's feet. Cloth that Bengé had been wearing.

A weird, stifled laugh struck the nape of D's neck. "You surprise me, you fearsome man. Were I anyone else, you'd have sliced me in two."

D didn't move. Even with his ultra-keen senses, he couldn't tell where Bengé was. As the saying went, Bengé's voice came out of thin air.

"Well, then," Bengé said, "I guess it's my turn now."

D's right hand moved ever so slightly. Two flashes of light gleamed, and sparks flew from the base of D's neck with the most beautiful sound. Bengé had stabbed down at D with a dagger after he suddenly materialized behind the Hunter, and the sparks resulted from that dagger being parried by the sword that flew back with just a simple movement of the Hunter's hand.

The tip of D's sword swept horizontally as he spun about, but there was no sign of Bengé. D kicked off the ground. Leaping five yards, as soon as he touched down he leapt again. Unable to detect anyone, he touched back down from his second leap. And then he heard it.

"Heh heh heh . . . It's no use, no use at all," Bengé's voice laughed. "As long as *the other you* is here, I'll be here, too."

In the forest ahead of him, a shadow rose silently. D's left hand raced into action, becoming white lightning blazing through the air. But the wooden needle he'd launched only nailed a length of thin black cloth to a nearby tree trunk. Beyond the tree, another shadow arose.

Is that an invitation? the Hunter thought. *Fine.* D sprinted into the woods. An invitation to follow him from the road to the woods—just what did Bengé have in mind?

The hot, humid atmosphere pressed him mercilessly from all sides. A sharp sound ripped through the wind. The silvery streaks that flew in rapid succession from either side of D were batted aside, one and all, by his blade.

"Oh, my. Not bad at all." Bengé's voice had a ring of admiration that wasn't in the least bit exaggerated.

"You said as long as I was here, you'd be here, didn't you?" D said without concern. There was no gloating over how he'd just thwarted the vicious attacks. "I see now. I know what your power is—"

"What?!" Bengé shouted. His daggers flew, as if to cover his shock and indignation. One came from straight ahead, the other from a thicket far to the rear of D—and they were nearly simultaneous. Did the Hunter face multiple opponents?

Deflecting the attacks with ease, D bent down. The instant a flash of white whizzed over his head, he swung his left hand back behind him. He could feel the rough wooden needle it held bite into flesh.

There was a cry of pain.

Taking an easy step forward, D then did something strange. As he turned back to whatever he'd just stabbed, he jabbed another needle into the ground at his feet at the same time. "What's wrong?" he said. "Until that needle gets pulled out, you can't get into my shadow, can you?"

It sounded like someone was grinding their teeth, and then something fell to the ground. A wooden needle stained with blood. It'd been tossed *up* from a patch of ground where there was nothing at all. Thrown out of the shadow of a tree barely cast on the ground by twilight.

As long as you're here, I'm here, he told D. *If you concentrate, you can see me. You don't see me because you think you can't*—that was the secret he'd imparted to Leila.

Bengé lurked in the shadows. But that wasn't all. His skill was such that even D couldn't detect his presence when he'd slipped into the Hunter's shadow. What's more, the way his attacks came from utterly impossible angles suggested he required no time at all to migrate from one patch of shade to the next. The slight delay between attacks was actually just the time it'd take to aim and throw a dagger. Once he'd slipped into his foe's shadow, he became an invincible assassin. So long as that foe wasn't D.

"Stanched the bleeding, have you? Too bad the fog is moving in," said D. Before he'd finished speaking, a dense white flow rolled in from the depths of the woods and boiled up at his feet. The twilit region lost its light.

Without light, no shadows can form.

D alone saw it. He saw the figure on the ground some ten feet ahead, clinging to the earth like a veritable sheet of black cloth. Their duel was as good as decided.

But at that instant the shadow tossed up a tiny ball of light. A blinding brilliance filled the milky white world, and the trees threw shadows across the ground.

"This time you have me beat. But we'll meet again," Bengé shouted, his pained parting words ringing from deep in the forest.

D slipped out of the woods and got on his horse. Within a few hours, he'd be within range of his target.

II

Hmph. Bengé isn't as great as he makes himself out to be. Looks like he got whipped," Mashira spat after he'd taken his ear from the ground and raised his head.

"As I expected, it was too much for him to handle, was it not?" It was Mayerling who said this. He, Mashira, and Caroline had camped out for the night in the middle of the forest, deciding that it would best to await Bengé's return.

Drifting around them was the savory aroma of birds cooking over the camp fire, skewered on sticks. Mashira reached out for one and offered it to Mayerling. "Would you care for some?"

"No."

"Suit yourself. The Nobility have no need for meat, right?" The Barbarois bodyguard said this as if he'd known that all along, but that was a lie. Somewhere in his tone there was malice. Mashira tore into the golden brown flesh, stuffing his cheeks. His yellowed teeth continued shredding the meat with a vulgar sound.

Not giving her compatriot so much as a glance, Caroline gazed at Mayerling's profile. Perhaps she'd eaten something already, for she ignored Mashira's roasting fowl. Not exactly the eyes of one in love, hers were feverish and clouded with passion.

"If he failed, the enemy will be after us. They'll catch us if we stay around here waiting. We'd best set off at once." Perhaps angered by Mashira's rude behavior, Mayerling's tone was enough to chill the blood. He turned abruptly from the fire.

"Please put your mind at ease," Caroline told him. "Our enemy won't be here any time soon. Not if he's pursuing a different carriage."

"A different carriage?" Mayerling asked as he turned to face them again.

"Correct," she replied. "A shadow carriage, if you will. It's one of Bengé's skills. Once someone begins chasing it, they'll never catch it a million years."

"I'm sorry to say I have no faith in the skills of one already bested in battle," said the Noble. "It occurs to me now that perhaps retaining the three of you was a mistake."

"What are you trying to say?" Caroline asked in an agitated manner. "I'll thank you kindly not to judge the abilities of the two of us unsatisfactory merely because the likes of Bengé proved a failure. Oh, that Bengé is an idiot. We would've been better served to let that damned Hunter go on pursuing us." Beneath her vermilion lips, her white teeth ground together.

"You'll see our true power, and I don't just mean someday. Perhaps as early as tomorrow. I believe there's another pack of bloodhounds on your heels."

"Yes, Mashira's right," said Caroline. "Tomorrow, I shall join forces with Bengé and slay every last one of those dogs, mark my words."

"I leave it to you then," Mayerling told her. "But tonight, we move out. Our destination is close at hand. We should be there the evening after next. A good time for our departure. I'm going on ahead. You two follow behind. By day I shall be sleeping in the forest."

Before long, the shrill sound of the wagon faded away, and the pair who had bowed as they'd seen the carriage off raised their heads.

Smiling faintly, Mashira said, "What right does a Noble doomed to extinction have to order around the famed Mashira, when my skill is known throughout the village of the Barbarois?"

"That can't be helped. He's our employer. We simply have to do our job." As Caroline spoke, she watched the departing carriage with a feverish gaze.

With a more lascivious smile, Mashira asked her, "Are you in love? With him?"

"Whatever do you mean by—"

"You don't have to hide it. He's the real thing. You're a *fake*. It's not like I can't see why that would attract you."

"Hold your tongue!" Caroline bared her teeth. Were those sharp canines she had peeking out between her lips? No—she couldn't be one of *those*.

"So, we've established that then. I have a proposal." Mashira smiled without a trace of fear, putting his best face on for the beautiful woman watching him with flame-like eyes.

"What would that be?"

"We've disobeyed the Elder," said Mashira. "Might we not be better off if we now discarded the standards those in the village live by?" For an instant it looked like she might turn on him for this unexpected overture, but then an excited expression arose on Caroline's face. "Oh, so I see the same thing had occurred to you," he continued. "If we stick to the rules of the village, then he's our employer, as you said. We mustn't disobey him, or turn on him. Lusting after him would be absolutely unthinkable. However, if we were to ignore the rules . . . "

Mashira's gaze was probing her face as he spoke, and at his words Caroline's eyes glittered piercingly. They were the eyes of an apostate who'd set her heart on discord.

"I thought you'd see it my way," the Barbarois man continued. "The only reason he won't so much as look at a gorgeous woman like you is because he's got a girl he loves, and who loves him, too. To tell the truth, I fancy the girl. I want to make her mine. Under the circumstances, wouldn't you say our interests coincide?"

She said nothing.

"During the day, he'll be sleeping. Maybe the girl will, too. If I were to take her and run off while he slept, he'd have no one left to rely on by day but you. Why, she's no more than a slip of a human girl. Could one of the Nobility seriously give his heart to that? He's already beginning to have a change of heart. Do you really think he'd go looking for her? Even supposing he does, once I've shown him proof I've had her myself, I guarantee you he'd be over their so-called eternal love," Mashira snickered.

"You have a point there." The flames painted grotesque shadows on Caroline's pale countenance. "But if I am to take him, body and soul, every last one of the lowly Hunters pursuing him must be slain. Even if the baron was mine, I could never sleep at ease if even one remained. If I agree to cooperate with what you propose, we shall have to leave both our charges alone and do our duty until we can take care of all the others. How does that strike you?"

"Fine by me," Mashira said with a nod.

"What of Bengé? Does he live?" asked Caroline.

"Well, I can't really say. He was certainly alive up till the point he used his shadow skills . . . You plan on letting him in on this?"

"That should go without saying! Once day breaks, I'll go off on a preemptive strike against the scum chasing us, and I'll try to locate our Bengé at the same time."

†

And where was D while these two ne'er-do-wells were plotting treachery against their charge? He was galloping down the road, through the fog, on a straight line from the spot where he'd encountered Bengé. In the haze to either side he could see shadowy images of the forest.

From up ahead, the wind carried something back. The creaking of a carriage. The range was about a mile and a quarter. On a night that could only be described as silent, could D's ears catch sounds from such a great distance?

His horse's hoofs beat the earth with increased impetus. The fog became a wall blocking him, then eddied away. Before long, a black carriage became visible ahead. There was no sign of the escorts.

D made a break forward. Even if the escorts had been there, he would have ridden forward without fear. On the far side of the carriage roof he could see only the driver's head. He was lashing away with a whip. D's right hand went to the sword on his back.

The distance continued to diminish. Perhaps the Hunter's approach had been noticed, for the whip danced wildly now. The gap between them widened slightly, and then rapidly grew. This would've been out of the question at the vehicle's usual speed. It seemed impossible that the most renowned steed, even with a legendary rider, would be able to keep on their tail now.

The carriage changed direction. Leaving in its wake a tortured squeal like its bolts were ready to pop free, it went into the woods to the right. It already had a lead of half a mile. And still the gap continued to grow.

D's heels pounded the flanks of his horse. Gradually, the dhampir's eyes began to give off a phosphorescent glow. He shredded the fog, and the gap shrank.

D came up alongside the carriage. Easily standing atop his saddle, he leapt for the carriage roof. It was as if all movement had been reduced to slow motion as D landed feet first on the roof of the vehicle. Crouching down, he advanced on the driver's seat. Ripples of suspicion crossed his face. The driver made no attempt to look his way, but worked the whip mechanically through the air. D's hand seized the supple lash. Even after it'd been taken away, the driver tried to crack the whip.

D set his right hand on the driver's hair. The instant he tugged back, the Hunter was tossed into the air by a violent shock. Incredibly, the hair in his hand, the carriage, and the horses all became a sheet of black cloth that fell to the ground, and D alone, completely ensnared by the inertia of their forward momentum, was thrown through the air.

Just as he was about to slam against the earth, the hem of his coat spread like a gigantic pair of wings, and D turned an easy somersault before landing feet first on the ground.

He gazed at the black cloth he held in his right hand. It cascaded across the ground, stretching another six feet. If spread out, there was enough to cover the floor of a small room. It must've taken a piece at least that large in order to make a carriage and driver, plus a half-dozen horses.

Discarding the cloth, D turned his face to the sky. He'd heard a voice from nowhere in particular cursing. Bengé's voice. D gazed at the sky in silence. In the east, beyond a range of mountain, a faint and watery light was beginning to shine. Surely the phantom carriage had been leading him in the wrong direction to buy Mayerling some time to escape. In terms of distance, it'd bought them perhaps an extra three-quarters of a mile. Racing at full speed, it'd take D less than two minutes to make that up.

Not bothering to search for the source of the disembodied voice, D straddled his horse without a word and galloped off. He was headed west, to where the sun sinks.

†

For the last ten or twenty minutes, the man had sat on a chair in the center of the dilapidated shop, his eyes shut tight. Dressed in black, the man was as thin as a half-starved crane. The sweat coating not only his brow but his whole body was not due solely to the stream of blood spilling from his flank—it also seemed connected to an extended period of concentrated mental effort.

When a faint blueness streamed into the dust-and-grit-covered shop, which was apparently a saloon, the man's whole body quaked, and his eyes bulged open. A scream of "Damn!" spilled from his mouth. Letting the tension drain from his body, the man slumped back in the chair in disappointment.

"Seems I underestimated him—the damn freak. Can't believe he caught up to my shadow carriage," he muttered. "Well, since I've blown it, I'd better let Mashira and the others know as soon as possible . . . " Wearily getting to his feet, Bengé trod across the dusty floor and left the shop.

On either side of a street only the wind ever crossed, ruined houses stood in rows. The hotel, the drugstore, the cobbler, the saloon he'd just come out of—every single shop had broken window panes with gaping black maws, and the signs above the doors swung idly. It was a ghost town.

Here in this town, less than a mile and a quarter from where he'd fought D, Bengé had done his very best to see to his wounds and to manipulate his shadow carriage. Coming to the center of the street, Bengé took a long, thin tube from the breast of his black robe, pulled the ring at one end, and thrust it up over his head. An orange ball of light shot from it, rising with a long tail behind it, and presently it could be seen no more. Shortly thereafter, a dazzling ring of light blazed in the heavens, maintaining that brilliance for a few seconds before it faded away.

"I sure hope they notice that and come for me," he muttered anxiously. When he started toward the horse tethered in front of the saloon, he heard the sound of hoofbeats and a car engine coming from one end of the long, central street.

Without even time to hide his horse, Bengé leapt across the street into the shadow of what looked to be a cyborg horse repair center. He had to wait but a few seconds for the body of a bus he'd seen before to appear from the other end of the street. The drivers must've installed some sort of non-reflective glass in it, because he couldn't see through the windshield.

The wheels ground to a halt right in front of the saloon, the door opened, and a pair of men stepped out. It was the guys he'd toyed with on the road through the mountains a day earlier. Hunters after Mayerling.

A killing-lust welled up, filling Bengé's entire being. The shadows of the buildings fell across the street. Between them and the men's shadows lay open ground. "Come on. Closer. Come to Bengé," he muttered to himself. If even part of one of their shadows touched that of the building where he concealed himself, he could slip into theirs in an instant. He'd become Death, invisible and inescapable.

The giant who called to mind a rock drew closer, with bow and arrows in hand. For an instant his shadow touched that from the tip of the roof of a building. Bengé's form faded away. The younger Hunter set his eyes on the other side of the street, and, when the giant changed direction and the shadow spun to his rear, the shade-like figure in black that silently rose behind the bigger man had the base of its neck covered with what looked like fine silvery feathers.

Faster than the giant's arrows in their indiscriminate flight, a swish of white knifed through the Barbarois' body as it first reeled back with an anguished cry, then went quickly into a face-first drop. Sending black blood out in all directions, Bengé's body split in half just above the waist. The two parts of his body quickly thudded to the ground.

"Is this the guy, Leila?" Borgoff called in the direction of the bus as he checked out the back of the enemy's head and its glistening feathers—needles from the sliver gun.

The driver's window slid open, and Leila's face and the leveled sliver gun appeared. "Yep. I got my payback."

Anticipating that they'd run across the foe who'd attacked her earlier, she had the window open a crack from the very beginning and had kept her brothers covered. And, while Bengé had by no means forgotten about Leila, his scorn for a girl he'd abused once already and his overwhelming confidence in his own abilities had dug his grave.

"No doubt about it—this is one of the threesome Grove mentioned. What the high hell was he doing out here?" Kyle said, spitting on the corpse.

"Dammit, how am I supposed to get any sleep now," Borgoff muttered. "Well, we've killed one of them, at any rate. Where I see he's got a horse tied up there and all, I'd say he's the only one here. But just to be sure, check out the area. Once we know it's clear, we'll take a little break, then head out again."

"Hold on, Borgoff. Can we afford to take it easy? We gotta gain all the ground we can while the sun shines," Leila called out from the window, but Borgoff swept her words away with one hand.

"See, he's got two drivers now that daylight don't bother. Besides, we've heard that it's the Claybourne States he's headed for. Well, if that's the case, I know a couple of routes we can take to head them off, so there's no need to get all flustered. To the contrary, I wouldn't mind letting D go on ahead to see if that Noble and him can't kill each other. I say it's a lucky thing we hit this town looking to bed down under a roof for a change."

Naturally, the oldest brother didn't catch the shade of emotion that rushed into Leila's face at the mention of D's name.

"Still, bro," Kyle began, as he used a finger to wipe the gore from his crescent blade, "you know, a long time ago, that the Claybourne States used to be a space port. There ain't nothing there but rows and rows of trashed rockets. What the hell could they—No, you don't think they could be planning to go to another planet, do you? Maybe for their honeymoon?!"

Even as she heard Kyle explode in laughter, Leila shut the window.

†

T he road was constantly bombarded by the chirping of little birds from the woods to either side.

In the spring sunlight, D raced on. Compared to when he'd chased the shadow carriage, his speed had decreased somewhat, but that was unavoidable. D's rein handling forced the cyborg horse to gallop at speeds far exceeding its abilities. The knee joints, metabolizers, and other parts already exhibited signs of severe stress. There was some question as to whether the horse would last another twelve hours, even if D eased back to his usual pace.

He had no choice but to wait for a nearby village or motorized mobile shop, but that was a faint hope.

The time was eight Morning. Could he catch up to Mayerling's carriage now that it could run by day as well? The prospects looked bleak. Still, he had to go on. It is the destiny of the huntsman to chase his prey.

How would his opponent react? Surely the Noble was aware that D and the Marcus clan were in pursuit. There was no way the Noble would just keep running. He'd definitely strike back at them. But when, and how?

Aside from the obvious psychological edge, those giving chase weren't necessarily always at an advantage when both parties were on the move. If the pursuers ran into an ambush, the tables could be turned. And there was nothing fiercer than cornered prey baring its fangs in its own defense.

The features of the young Noble skimmed across D's heart. The Noble wasn't lying when he said he wouldn't do anything to the human. D could almost picture the face of the girl in the carriage, and the look she'd have in her eyes.

The scenery before him suddenly changed. Gone was the constant greenery, replaced by a rough desert plain. In various places, the land was fused into a glassy state, and eye-catching machines and vehicles of titanic proportions jutted from the ground. There were heaps of pitiful, mechanical corpses left on the field, each and every one red and crumbling with rust. They seemed to stretch on to the ends of the earth, and the disturbing, ghastly air they had about them didn't seem in the least bit like that of anything mechanical. When night came, would the bitter voices of single-minded machines echo pathetically across the plain?

This was one of the ancient battlefields where, long ago, machines that'd evolved into sentience fought each other out of hatred. Even now, a number of them still hadn't ceased functioning, their bodies squirming around on a pale and feeble current, wandering night after night in search of their enemies.

The ambush could come any time now. That was the feeling D had. As day broke, he'd seen the flash of what seemed to be a Hunter's signal flare in the dawn sky to the rear. Undoubtedly it was the signal from Bengé, reporting his mission had failed and that D was still in pursuit. Of course, the remaining pair of guards would see it and take the necessary countermeasures. The question was, would some of the party keep moving? Both of the Barbarois probably wouldn't come after him, but one of them might attack.

Then there was the other group to consider. No doubt the Marcus clan had noticed the flare, too. They had much more detailed knowledge of this area. There was every reason to worry about them taking some little-known shortcut to head off the carriage. And, in the world of day, swimming with the song of life, even D couldn't possibly hear their footfalls. Would they let him go on ahead? Or would he fall prey to one of their ambushes?

D's face clouded ever so slightly. Perhaps he'd been thinking about the youngest, the little sister. About the girl with the big, round eyes who said she couldn't live any other way but as a Hunter. If she let her hair down instead of pulling it back she'd probably look a good two years younger. With a touch of rouge to her cheeks and some lipstick, she could pass for a regular girl from any old town. She wouldn't have to cry out for her mother, tortured by fever.

D's countenance lost its shade of humanity. Far ahead of him, he'd sighted a toppled column of mammoth proportions. Running in a straight line across the fifteen-foot-wide road was a gigantic, rusted forearm.

†

Just before D had intruded on the ancient battlefield, there'd been a woman by the side of the road in what was just about the center of this vast expanse of land. She was combing her hair in the morning breeze. The dress she wore was bluer than the bluest sky, and the voice spilling from her lips in song was as beautiful as any jewel. If only she didn't have those spiteful red lips. However, a black shadow fell clearly across the cylindrical generator against which the woman was leaning. The demons of the night weren't supposed to have shadows.

It was unclear how long she'd been there, but the woman seemed to be absorbed in toying with the golden thread that was her hair. Suddenly, she looked up. Her gaze went in the direction from which D's hoofbeats echoed.

"Ah, someone's coming," the woman—Caroline—laughed, but her rose-like beauty soon grew tense. "Those hoofbeats don't sound like any human's horse. It's D. Now there's a man to be feared . . . "

Even now, the image of D's swordplay in the village of the Barbarois was burned into Caroline's retinas. But, an instant later, her blue eyes blazed with a lust for blood and battle. A smile warped her ruby lips.

"It seems it was worthwhile waiting here to get some rest and lay an ambush. I will make this your grave . . . "

And, with that muttered declaration of war, Caroline scanned the surrounding machinery, nodded once, then approached one of the devices. Rust coated its surface, and a number of jumbled pipes ran out of it. Caroline laid her hands on one of those closest and nestled it lovingly to her cheek, but, before long, her expression grew terribly lurid. Her mouth opened. Inside, her mouth was the same bloody red as her lips. Two of her canines were exposed, and, when they came in contact with the rusty pipe, the tips sank effortlessly into the metal.

Slowly, twin streams slid down Caroline's luscious throat, leaving a damp trail as they coursed to her ample bosom. The beauty's throat pulsated, and she drank as if ravenous. Over and over, gulp after gulp.

Before long, Caroline pulled back, and the fluid leaking from the holes mysteriously stopped. The Barbarois woman stepped away from the machine like a petal drifting off in the breeze. Showered with sunlight, her red tongue played along her lips. "Ah, that's what I like," she purred. "Now listen well to what I have to say."

The machine moved. Painfully slow. Its five fingers clawed at the sand. Each digit at least a yard long. Measuring thirty feet overall, the device she'd chosen was a robotic forearm that'd been broken off at the elbow.

†

D halted his steed. The arm was sixty feet away. It was like an exquisite piece of sculpture; even the shapes of the muscles and the lines of blood vessels remained discernible through the rust.

While the great machine battles had primarily been contests of combat ability, a sort of conflict between bizarre aesthetic sensibilities had also existed. In response to the geometrical orderliness of their rivals—epitomized by designs that were conglomerations of planes and spheres simplified to the extreme— some uncouth machines had taken the imitation of the human form to a level of beauty and perfection surpassing even the classic artistry of antiquity. Whether or not true "artists" existed among the machines, they not only accurately reproduced human hair on their androids, but every last pore as well.

Unofficial historical accounts kept by the Nobility reserved a special place for the earth-shaking contest between Apollo, with a thirty-foot sword in hand, and Hercules, armed with three hundred feet of spear. The surpassing destructive power unleashed in their clash changed the shape of mountains, wiped away valleys, and stopped the course of rivers. Had the limb now blocking D's path belonged to one of those famed combatants, or was it a remnant of some nameless Goliath?

A figure in blue frolicked on top of the wrist. The morning breeze rustled her golden hair and bore the aroma of her sweet perfume. Only D could detect something else. The foul stench of blood that drifted with it. "I am Caroline of the Barbarois," she said. "And I can let you go no further."

In D's pupils, which reflected only a void, the woman's image laughed coldly. Her body swayed wildly. The arm beneath her feet jolted as it changed direction, pointing toward D. Power coursed into the fingers, and they dug into the soil. Once they were embedded, the arm used them as a fulcrum and started to slide forward like an inchworm. It moved roughly, but with surprising speed.

D was motionless. Perhaps the surreal phenomenon of this rusted arm coming to life had robbed him of his nerve.

When the arm had come within fifteen feet of him, spread its fingers wide, and slammed against the earth, D charged on his horse. The colossal arm hung in midair. It'd sprung into the air from the force of the fingers striking the ground. D might've discerned the time and location of impact from its position, because, as the titanic arm's ten-foot-wide palm made the earth tremble, he slipped out from under it by a hair's breadth.

The fingers slammed shut, tearing up soil. Turning toward D, it lifted just its wrist until it was perpendicular to the ground. The fingers were still clenched. When it flopped forward, it opened them at last. A brown mass flew straight for D and his horse, more than sixty feet away. That distance rapidly diminished.

Perhaps feeling the air pressure to their rear, D tugged the reins to the right. As his horse went a few lengths in that direction, the mass dropped at its feet. It was the soil itself, the same soil that'd been gouged out by the fingers—a fitting projectile for a colossal arm.

Catching the shock wave on its flank, the horse lurched to one side. D danced through the air. Like a veritable mystic bird he flew, landing in a spot some five yards away. His horse regained its balance and dashed back to him.

The colossal arm set its sights on D. It came after him with terrific speed, making the earth tremble. A black fingertip passed right before D's eyes as the Hunter leapt backward. His stone-cold face remained impassive as a cloud of sand struck it.

"What's the matter, Hunter?" Caroline laughed charmingly from atop the arm. "Can't do a thing, can you? You see, this arm has joined the ranks of the undead."

Hard as it was to believe, the arm did have a power plant in the wrist, and it ran on gasoline. And Caroline had sucked some of the remaining fuel from the pipe. This "vampire" had taken what was akin to the "blood" of the colossal arm. Those bitten by the accursed demons became demons themselves. But it hardly seemed possible that the same abominable rule would extend to a mechanical arm.

The colossal forearm was now one of the living dead, a corpse that moved in accordance to Caroline's will. It didn't seem possible that even D could repel these attacks forever, when one followed another with such blistering speed.

In accordance with instructions from Caroline, the arm had chased D right over to the horizontal wreckage of a gigantic torso. Though the body was toppled, the side was still easily thirty feet high, a distance even D couldn't possibly jump.

"Are you finished, Hunter?" Caroline asked, tittering uncontrollably. "The sword upon your back—is it a mere affectation?"

With his rear blocked off, D appeared unable to do anything, and the wrist rose up over his head. A black brilliance surged up from the ground, slipped between the fingers crushing down now like an avalanche, and settled on top of the mechanical arm.

"What?!" Caroline exclaimed. D's coat flashed elegantly right in front of her as her eyes widened in amazement.

"Now we're even," the Hunter said softly.

Thinking to say something in return, Caroline took a few steps back—toward the elbow—as if she'd been pushed back by some unsettling emanations invisible to the eye. The colossal arm stopped dead in its usual inchworm pose. Beads of sweat rose on Caroline's brow. The beads immediately grew larger, coursing down her paraffin skin. The sunlight made the wet streaks glitter like quicksilver.

Both of D's arms hung naturally by his sides.

Various ideas whirled through Caroline's head. There wasn't enough room to flee. And the first time they'd met, Caroline had realized this youth wasn't the sort who'd spare her because she was a woman.

D took a step forward.

"W . . . wait," Caroline said desperately, humiliated by the way her voice quavered. "Even if you slay me, Mashira still remains. Wouldn't you like to know about his powers?" Cornered now, it was the best plan her brain could conceive. For a warrior, learning the abilities of the next opponent they'd meet in combat was more important than anything else. This offer would sway him without fail.

D advanced another step.

"Wait, just wait." Caroline waved her hands and leapt back a few yards. So, this youth gave no consideration to knowledge that might give him the advantage in battle? *I'm going to die, aren't I?* Caroline thought. *Here, on this man's sword . . .* Caroline gazed absentmindedly at the youth in black raiment approaching her. A strange feeling welled up in her breast. *I want to be slain. I want to feel this gorgeous man stab into my bosom.* The ecstasy of death enveloped Caroline in its rapture.

D's movements ceased. Letting out a low moan, the figure in black fell to one knee.

Not knowing quite what'd happened, Caroline instinctively went into action, seeking life instead of death. The colossal arm flipped over, leaving the two of them to drop through thin air. Still, D managed a spectacular landing before one of his knees buckled again. The colossal arm fell toward him. There wasn't enough time to get out of the way.

D's right hand blurred. It looked like it smoldered. There was a flash of silver that intersected the fingers crushing down on him like an avalanche of digits. With a tremendous crash, the foot-and-a-half-thick middle finger fell behind D, and everything else from the wrist forward twisted back. Black streams of machine oil poured down from the wound-like rent in the metal.

At the same time, Caroline landed on the opposite side of the road. She pressed down on the fingers of her right hand and grew pale. There was a thin vermilion line around the base of them.

D leapt. His cyborg horse was under him.

"I'm not letting you get away, Hunter," Caroline cried out. With streams of black oil trailing from it, the trembling hand went into a deadly pounce.

D was moving at a gallop. Could he escape?

The colossal arm went after the horse and rider. Flames suddenly blossomed from the mechanical wrist, traveling all the way to the elbow. Melting in the heat of a nuclear missile—which could reach a hundred thousand degrees—the abhorred demon arm collapsed to the ground as little more than a burning log of steel.

The smoke trails of five missiles hung in the air. From back down the same road that'd brought D, there reverberated the sounds of a nimble engine. The low-profile vehicle with huge puncture-proof tires was, needless to say, the battle car. And Leila was at the wheel.

After killing that master of the shadows, Bengé, Leila had wrangled herself a scouting mission by saying she couldn't help wondering what their foes were up to. When she left, she said

she'd be right back, but an hour had passed, then three. She'd gone searching for D.

Her brothers said the freaks were probably lying in wait for him. They laughed about how sweet it'd be if they all killed each other. And the more Leila thought about how likely they were to be right, the larger the face of that gorgeous young man so full of the void loomed in her heart. *That's just because he saved my life twice*, she thought. But Leila had never been given to thoughts about repaying debts before. If she collapsed from hunger and someone gave her food, she'd have had no compunctions about pulling a knife on her savior to steal the rest from him. That's simply how Leila—and all of the Marcus clan—did things. The very concept of returning a favor was alien to them. But as Leila held the yoke of the battle car and ripped through the morning air, her heart held the closest thing to it.

The instant she entered the ancient battlefield and saw the colossal arm chasing D, it was a movement of her heart rather than her conscious will that made her press the firing button and launch those miniature nuclear rockets. She didn't know that the colossal arm, writhing in pain from the loss of a finger, couldn't have caught up to D at the speed he galloped.

Stopping alongside the arm, which had ceased moving and spouted lotus-red flames, she scanned the area with her sharp gaze. She was searching for Caroline. But the freak was nowhere to be found. With a disappointed cluck of her tongue, Leila stepped on the gas.

†

Having ridden hard for about two miles, D veered off the road and into the forest. A horrendous torpor was sweeping over him. It was the sunlight syndrome, a condition unique to dhampirs. Inheriting half or more of a vampire's characteristics as they did, dhampirs could move about by day without concern, but that was not without its drawbacks. While they remained oblivious, a tenacious form of fatigue was building in their half-immortal flesh from the merciless rays of the sun. For dhampirs working as Hunters, the most dreaded aspect of this affliction was that the symptoms manifested without warning in the form of a sudden feeling of exhaustion and ever-increasing lassitude. It was painfully clear what would happen if someone were to suffer an attack of this while locked in deadly battle.

D's narrow escape couldn't really be called a retreat or a defeat. In fact, it was only thanks to D's superhuman strength that he was able to get himself in the saddle. But, when he got off his horse deep in the forest, D's gait was somewhat troubled.

The ground here was shrouded by multicolored flora and teeming with insect life. D knelt down and started to scoop at the dirt with a knife he pulled from his combat belt. Earth and moss flew with his intense movements. In less than three minutes, he had hollowed out a depression large enough for a person to lie in. With just the lightest shake of his head, D quietly entered the hole. Once he'd used his hands to pull the dirt around him onto his body, he laid back.

The reason vampires in legends of antiquity carried coffins filled with soil from their homeland was not merely because the grave they should've occupied offered them the most serene sleep. Actually, their kind had discovered in ancient times that Mother Earth would draw out the fatigue that accumulated in their bodies and instill them with new immortalizing energy. And D was following their example.

"Heh, this is a fine mess," D's left hand snorted. "Hell, even I can't tell you when the sunlight syndrome will strike. The fact that you're tougher than the average customer only makes matters worse. What's it been, five years or so?"

The voice from his hand must've been talking about how long it'd been since the last attack. Usually, those dhampirs who'd inherited the greater part of their disposition from the vampires went an interval of about six months between outbreaks of the symptoms. Using the date and time of the last one as a rough base, they'd hide themselves for a month before and after the next expected attack, avoiding all combat during that time. These precautions weren't solely out of fear of reprisals from the prey they chased, but also to avoid attacks from their business competitors. There were always plenty of scheming cowards looking for a larger share of the Hunting business, and they'd keep elaborate records of the dates their rivals had attacks, then try to learn their whereabouts before the next one was due so they could do away with them. Needless to say, in D's case, he'd have to guard against a fierce onslaught by Caroline and her cohorts.

"Well, looks like we're on vacation for a while. Good luck," the voice said. But by the time these carefree comments rose from his left hand, D's eyes were already closed.

Journey's End

CHAPTER 5

I

While D and Caroline's deadly encounter was unfolding on the ancient battlefield, Mayerling's jet-black carriage was parked on the shore of a lake some forty miles away as the crow flies. The sky was clear and blue, the trees by the shore benefited from the abundant water, and rainbows seemed to spring from every leaf and twig. Far off, a blue mountain range capped with white snow stretched into the distance, and golden birds skimmed the peaks. As scenery went, this was a truly beautiful and placid tableau.

As he watered the horses on the lake shore, a serious expression flitted into Mashira's wicked visage, as if he were mulling something over. He'd been that way since a short while earlier—when he'd parted company with Caroline. Now, waiting for the horse to finish drinking, he seemed to be gazing intently at the ugly face reflected in the water. Finally, after some minutes of rapt concentration, he muttered, "Okay," and slapped his hands together. Following that, he stooped to pick a number of the white flowers blooming by the shore. As he started walking toward the carriage parked a little way off, a charitable expression, strangely free from worry, arose on his face.

He tapped on a window with shades tightly drawn, and a voice over an intercom answered with an inquisitive, "Yes?" At this charmingly plaintive voice, he stopped the unconscious licking of his lips, and, in an amiable tone, he replied, "I was wondering if you wouldn't like to open the window and get a breath of fresh air. The sky is blue, the water clear, and the whole place is filled with the sweet scent of flowers. Though milord Mayerling slumbers, I believe you have nothing to fear so long as Mashira is here."

There was no reply. Behind the window, she must have been hesitating.

Perhaps seeing some spark of hope, Mashira said as buoyantly as he could, "Here, look how beautiful the flowers are. The ground's completely covered with them. If you're that worried, just open the shade and drink in their color if you will."

There was silence again, and, just as he was deciding his ploy wasn't going to work, the black shutter shot up smoothly. Seeing her innocent face quietly peering out like a moonflower, Mashira smiled inside.

How can I get her to come out here? That's the question that'd wracked his brain since before they had arrived at the lake. He'd considered a number of options, but, in the end, he decided to exploit the feelings she was bound to have as a young human girl. Even if she was with her boyfriend, even if he'd expressly told her not to go outside, there was no way a maiden of her tender years wouldn't want a breath of fresh air after being cooped up in a carriage for days. After all, the darkness was no place for a human to live. Ever since Mashira had taken Mayerling's place at the reins at dawn, he had schemed of using the girl's humanity to his advantage. Planning ahead, he took the carriage off the road and steered it to this remote locale.

"Say, how do you like these?" Mashira quickly thrust the bunch of flowers he'd concealed behind his back against the windowpane.

The girl's eyes became terribly blurred, and her white hand reached out. It bounced off the windowpane in vain.

"What are you waiting for? What's the harm in merely stepping out for bit of fresh air?" And then Mashira became even more empathic. "The flowers are in bloom, birds are singing, and when this place seeps into your pores and makes you even happier, milord Mayerling is certain to thank me for a job well done. And of course, the purse for our contract might gain a little weight, as well. Think of it, if you will, as your way of helping out one poor bodyguard."

The girl's eyebrows knit with reflection. In less time than it took to draw a breath, her pupils sparkled and the door handle spun. The girl stepped down into the meadow, and the darkness of the interior was scattered by the sunlight.

His beautiful prey had finally played into the trap. Gently taking her by the hand, Mashira led her to the shore.

"It's so beautiful," the pretty young lady exclaimed, proving that she was indeed a resident of the world of daylight. Where the little waves encroached on the shore, the girl knelt and reached out to touch the surface of the lake. Ripples spread, obscuring her gorgeous countenance. Pulling back the hand she'd put wrist-deep in the water, she searched for a handkerchief to wipe her face. The surface of the lake returned to calmness.

Mashira was standing behind her. The front of his gray coat was open. Maybe the girl glimpsed something inside it, because she froze without saying a word. When she finally turned and Mashira's hands grabbed her by both shoulders, something brown and tube-like stretched between their abdomens with unholy speed . . . out of Mashira's gut and toward the girl. The girl squirmed, but Mashira's hands never left her. Her well-formed body was pushed down into the brush without any real effort.

"What are you doing? Let me go!"

"Can't do that," Mashira said, grabbing the hand the girl levered against his jaw and twisting it up. "I'm crazy about you," he continued. "You're gonna be mine. If you just take it you don't have to get hurt. I'll take care of that jerk Mayerling, too."

"What are you talking about? Let go. If you don't let go of me—"

"What'll you do? Out in the middle of the woods like this, you can shout but nobody will come. Now, why don't the two of us get to know each other a lot better . . . "

A mouth burning with desire tried to close on her lips, which trembled with fear and anger. It was then that intense gunfire resounded. As Mashira jerked up his head, there were tremendous explosions of pain in his jaw and crotch.

Grunting as she pushed his body off, the girl got up quickly. Behind the carriage, she spied what looked to be a huntsman with a still-smoking rifle thrown over his shoulder. There'd been someone around after all.

The girl quickly ran for the carriage. The huntsman cut her off. Unsettling shadows clung to his scraggily bearded face. "Missy, what in the blazes are you?" he asked.

"Excuse me?"

"Don't play dumb with me. This here carriage's gotta belong to the Nobility. Why on earth would you be trying to get into it?"

"The truth is . . . "

As the girl hemmed and hawed, the huntsman threw a vulgar laugh her way. Suddenly, he grabbed her chin with one hand. With his substantial strength, the man exposed first one side of the girl's neck, then the other. "No wounds . . . meaning you hooked up with a Noble of your own accord, didn't you? You little traitor. Once I've taken care of that bastard, I'll learn you a thing or two. And when you've known a real man's touch, I'll send you to join your bloodsucker."

An unbelievably fierce gale was blowing in the girl's head. *This man means me harm, too,* she thought. *The moment I set foot outside of the carriage, I meet with one misfortune after another. Oh, if only I'd stayed with my love . . .*

"Get your hands off her," she heard Mashira say in a low but clear voice. Still smarting from the blow to his crotch, he remained somewhat hunched over as he came closer. His look had changed. He was so enraged now, almost nothing remained of his expression. "Get your stinking hands off her," he repeated.

"Ha! If you think you can make me, give it a shot," the huntsman laughed scornfully. "I figure chances are pretty good you're just a drifter who ran across this girl the same as me, but trying to rape her here was piss-poor planning. I'll be sure to nail her once for you, too, though. Now run along to hell." And, saying that, he threw the girl down in the opposite direction from the carriage and took the high-caliber gunpowder-rifle in his left hand.

"Wait just a—" Mashira started to say, but with an explosive bang like a hammer striking steel plate an enormous hole opened right in the middle of his heart. His hunched body was thrown back over six feet. A scream rose from the girl, and the air was clouded by a vermilion mist.

"Okay, now to deal with you," the huntsman chortled. "After I've had my share of fun with you, I'll drag you back to town for everyone to see." And with that the huntsman turned around, and an alarmed expression arose on his face. The girl's face had been flooded by a look of sheer terror. Following the path her eyes had taken, now it was the huntsman who froze.

Mashira was coming toward them. Covered with blood, a gaping hole in his chest where he'd taken the high-caliber shell. There was no need to see how his eyes had lost their light when the bloodless face was that of a corpse. The way he walked was strangely stiff. Almost as if it was something he wasn't accustomed to doing . . .

The huntsman shouted something. His rifle seemed to howl in response.

Mashira's head exploded like a watermelon. It may well have been that his steps became swifter at that point because his load had just been made that much lighter.

The huntsman couldn't move. The nerves that drove his body had withered to nothing when the rifle he placed so much stock in had proved ineffective.

The hands of the headless man reached out and grabbed hold of the huntsman's powerful shoulders. "You know, I was just getting used to this body. Now I'll take yours, you bastard." There wasn't even time to notice how this voice so unlike Mashira's reverberated from his belly before something like a brown tube sank into the huntsman's abdomen, rising from the same spot on the walking corpse.

Several seconds passed. For the girl, it was a nightmarish eternity.

"Heh heh heh—the transfer is complete," the voice said from his new belly. The belly of the huntsman, that is . . .

Without wasting time to watch the headless corpse tumbling to the ground, the girl, who'd long since reached her limit of horror, gave a scream and dashed off into the forest. Though the huntsman followed her with his eyes, for some reason he didn't set out after her. "There's no use in her trying to run," he snickered, "but I only gave her *a little of me*, so we're not quite ready to start either. Guess I might as well have myself a little game of hide-and-seek," he muttered, starting after her at a brisk pace.

†

When the last scrap of canned beef had been safely tucked away in his stomach, Kyle threw the empty can into the street. The cylinder rustled hollowly for several bounces and then, as it hung in the air on another, a silvery flash of light split it in two before zipping back to Kyle's waist.

It was the main street of the ghost town. Kyle was sitting on the edge of the boardwalk that jutted from the front of the saloon. When rain soaked streets like these, the mire could be difficult for pedestrians to negotiate.

Parked in front of the drugstore, the bus opened its door and Borgoff stuck his head out. He seemed on edge.

"What do you wanna do, bro?" Kyle asked, getting to his feet.

Borgoff made a concerned face. "Grove's had another attack," he said, looking up at the heavens. "A real bad one this time. His heart might not be able to take it."

"That ain't good. We still might need him to do his stuff one more time if something comes up." With a snort of laughter, he added,

"Maybe me and Leila went at it a little too hot and heavy for him."

"You moron," Borgoff bellowed, his face severe, but he soon folded his arms and donned a morose expression. "Of course, you probably ain't far wrong. I mean, we knew it wasn't any good for his health to force him to send his other self out like that," he muttered.

"Anyway, let's roll," said Kyle. "We'll lose the daylight if we hang around here waiting for freaking Leila. The Noble's making better time than we figured."

"Yep," Borgoff replied, but his face was dark.

This cruel clan had always managed to take care of not only the prey they stalked, but their competitors as well. But now they'd lost their brother Nolt, Leila hadn't returned, and even bedridden Groveck hovered near death.

Leila's failure to return didn't necessarily mean she'd been slain, but, in light of the strength of their foes, the brothers couldn't be sure. Worse yet, Borgoff harbored another fear about his little sister. That she'd fallen for D.

When they'd picked their sister up after she'd been injured in her first engagement with the Noble, every chunk of shrapnel had already been pulled out of her, and Leila was resting peacefully. They'd asked who'd patched her up, but she said she couldn't remember. It sure as hell wasn't the Noble. Which meant it had to be D. In fact, there were signs two other people had clashed near where they'd found Leila. She hadn't made any mention of that. But, given his sister's temperament, it wasn't inconceivable she'd keep it to herself. D was someone they were going to take out, after all. The fact that he'd saved her life would be nothing but pure humiliation.

However, Leila didn't seem in the least bit mortified. And that was just the start. Her expression was pained even while they strategized together, and she seemed strangely tired. Their clan wasn't so soft they'd make a big deal out of that, but her condition seemed to have nothing to do with physical exhaustion. Considering all the facts, Borgoff realized she'd only exhibited these signs whenever they discussed what to do about D. Putting two and two together, he thought, *Bingo!*

But in his heart of hearts, there was one thought Borgoff couldn't get rid of, peerless Vampire Hunter though he was—the question of whether it was really D that'd saved Leila after all. At that point, D must've known for a fact that the Marcus clan should be considered his enemy. By all accounts, he wasn't the kind of man to go easy on any armed opponent, woman or not. Even if half of what people said about D's abilities, his battles, and the list of foes he'd slain could be discounted as idle talk, the remainder was enough to send icy fingers up the nape of Borgoff's neck. *He of all people had saved Leila?* Borgoff found that hard to believe. And that's why he hadn't tried to stop his sister from going out on reconnaissance that morning.

Borgoff swept away the tangled knot of ideas. "Let's go," he said. "If Leila's okay, she'll send up a flare or get in touch with us one way or another."

The two of them got back on the bus. Kyle took the driver's seat, while Borgoff went into the bedroom. There wasn't a single breath to be heard from Groveck's bunk. Shriveled and dry like a mummy, you could've put your ear to his motionless chest and not even heard a heartbeat. Right now, *this* Groveck was indeed dead.

When Borgoff looked down at the lifeless husk of his youngest brother, a pained and human expression crept into his supremely fierce face, and then the bus shook a little as it began to move.

II

Two women were walking through the forest. One of them— a gorgeous, shapely blonde in a blue dress—headed deep into the forest with her eyes fixed on one spot straight ahead. The other—dressed in a light shirt and slacks—looked like she was just out for a stroll in the woods, but from time to time she stopped and checked the ground or looked at how the brush was broken before walking on a little further. Though her eyes kept scanning the forest, she didn't seem to be in the least bit lost. The eyes of both women sought the same thing. The young Vampire Hunter, defenseless in his makeshift grave.

Leila stopped and wiped the sweat from her brow. After she'd fried the colossal hand Caroline controlled, she'd gone right after D. She had no definite reason for doing so, but, judging by the way he'd run off, it was clear something was wrong with him. It wasn't like the great D to be nearly killed by a woman, no matter what sort of freak she might be. There was only one reason for that she could think of—sunlight syndrome.

He would've taken off for the forest then, seeking Mother Earth. It was easy enough to follow the hoofprints. She'd even found the spot where he'd slipped into the woods. That was where the trouble started. The battle car couldn't get through. Without regret, Leila had left her cherished vehicle behind.

She wasn't sure exactly what Caroline would do, but, judging by how the woman's strength compared to that of Leila's brothers or D, and in light of how much trouble she'd had trying to do away with the dhampir before, there was certainly a very good chance she'd be intent on killing D now. What's more, the Barbarois woman possessed strange powers. She might've already beaten Leila to D. It was so easy to kill a dhampir suffering from sunlight syndrome, it made the super-human abilities they displayed in their chosen profession seem like a distant dream.

With a javelin in her hand and the sliver gun shoved through her belt, Leila entered the forest. The hoofprints were fading fast, filled in by quickly growing moss. All she was left with were the instincts she'd refined in her life as a Hunter. The question was, would that be enough to make her a match for the Barbarois woman? Now that Leila had abandoned her beloved car, she'd be no more than a normal human girl to Caroline.

Bearing right for a few yards, she suddenly came into a clearing. She saw the horse tethered to the branch of a nearby tree. D lay half-buried in the dirt by the horse's feet. Choking back a cry of joy, she kicked up moss as she scrambled over to him.

There was nothing out of the ordinary. His beautiful countenance—which sufficed to give her goosebumps even at this distance—was supremely wise and enduringly stern, and his eyelids were closed as if he was deep in contemplation.

Leila's shoulders fell. Something hot spilled past her eyelids, to her great surprise. The last time she'd cried was a distant memory. She seemed to remember wiping away her tears by the side of a blood-stained old woman whose face she could clearly recall even now. *Who had that been?* she wondered.

Forcefully wiping her tears away, Leila laid herself down gently on top of D's dirt-covered body. It was so cold. The chill she felt wasn't from the soil. It was D's body temperature. When Kyle had come along and found her after she'd been wounded in her battle with the Noble, he told her she would've died out there if someone hadn't kept her warm. Of course there hadn't been a heating unit around. D had kept her warm.

It wasn't as if she'd never had feelings for anyone before. She'd been proposed to a number of times. But all her suitors had left when they found out what her last name was. All but one. Leila drove him off. Because that night, she'd been violated by her brothers.

"We're not letting you go anywhere," said Borgoff. Nolt whispered to her that he'd wanted to have his way with her for a long time. Kyle lost himself in the act without a word. As soon as the other three backed off and Groveck's nearly mummified form mounted her, something in Leila's soul flew away. And ever since, she'd been a colder killer than ever before.

But now that special something had returned.

"You saved me," Leila fairly whispered to the gorgeous, immobilized man. "This time, *I'll* protect *you.* I'll defend you with my life."

A strange presence moved through the woods. Checking that the safety of her sliver gun was off, Leila took the javelin in hand and let the fighting spirit fill her. She rose to her feet.

†

He was lying on a hill of pure green. As he rarely got to go outside, each time, short though it was, was absolute bliss. Joy bubbled like a fount in his heart. Gentle gusts of wind, showers of sunlight, the scent of dense tufts of new grass, the blue mountain range stretching toward eternity—all these things made him realize what a pleasure it was to be alive. *Now this is living!* he thought to himself.

It was Groveck, or rather, the "spirit" of Groveck that had escaped from the sickly body left in the Marcus bus. The sound of footsteps rose from the forest behind him. He turned to find a girl running toward him. The fear in her countenance spoiled his mood. Just when he was enjoying himself.

"Help! Please, help me," the girl cried out, circling around behind him.

He was perplexed. His forte was getting people to run away from him, not toward him. But the reason the girl had said what she did was soon apparent. Out of the woods stepped a man armed with a large rifle, apparently a huntsman of some sort.

The huntsman looked around restlessly, but soon spotted him and the girl. The huntsman approached them with powerful strides. Grove heard screams of fear spill out from behind his back. For the first time in his life, he felt something unprecedented stirring in his heart. The other man stopped about a yard away and swung the muzzle of the rifle to bear on him.

Grove was a bit surprised. Every inch of the huntsman's body brimmed with hostility and self-confidence. Though he'd never seen this other man before, it appeared the huntsman knew who he was. "What do you want?" he tried to ask, but the other man didn't seem to hear him, and not a muscle moved in his own face. That's the way it always went. He gave up on ordinary communication.

"Give me the girl," the man ordered. His voice was cold. Any fool could well imagine what would happen whether he complied with the huntsman's command or not.

"If you don't want to, fine," the huntsman added. "I mean, it's not like I'm gonna let you live anyway. Strange meeting you here, though."

Grove tilted his head. He just couldn't recall who this other man was. His opponent, however, was kind enough to provided the answer.

"But then, you wouldn't know me in this shape, now would you?" the huntsman snickered. "I was part of the threesome over next to the carriage when you snuck into the village of the Barbarois."

Learning this, Grove was no less bewildered. He could, indeed, recall the trio in question. However, that middle-aged man, jet-black youth, and shapely beauty were all quite different from the huntsman now before his eyes.

"Oh, that's right—I still haven't shown you my true face. The one you saw before, and this one I have now, are no more than temporary hosts. The real me looks like *this!*" And with that, the huntsman pulled up his shirt with one hand.

Grove let his mouth fall open. But there was nothing on the huntsman's belly. When the girl gasped, it was like the signal for the change. As they watched, a number of deep creases that couldn't really be called wrinkles coursed across the huntsman's abnormally protruding belly, and then what looked like a human face bulged from the surface, showing a little nose, lips like purple scraps of meat, and eyes that blinked wide open. The tips of the yellow teeth spilling over the twisted lips came to fang-like points. It was a tumor . . . a tumor that had a face like a person, and a life of its own. The body of the huntsman was no more than a vessel for it to move around in.

"Surprised, junior?" the tumor asked. "This is the real me. I've been hopping from body to body for five hundred years. It'll take a lot more than your tricks to beat me."

At last Grove grasped the situation. Hostility flooded into his heart. Perhaps it showed.

"Let's get one thing straight," the tumor laughed. "If you let your lightning fly, I'll shoot and the girl behind you will die, too. You got that?"

For a moment, Grove was befuddled.

The abdominal tumor added, "Of course, the girl's not exactly in pristine shape anymore. You ought to have a good look at her stomach."

The weird course of the conversation shifted Grove's attention to his rear. Before the fierce report of the gun could reach him, he was struck in the chest by heat and a forceful impact. Flying backward, he saw the blue sky. It seemed his foe had aimed away from the girl. He'd never had any intention of shooting her.

Without even glancing at the punk toppling backward in a bloody mist, the huntsman—that is to say, the eerie countenanced carbuncle—smiled at the girl. "Okay," he said, "come to me now. If that bastard Mayerling gets out and about, there'll be hell to pay. See, I'm not allowed to do anything to his coffin. So I want to get as far away from here as we can before darkness falls."

A relieved expression arose in the girl. Realizing at this point that she was worried about Mayerling's safety, the expression of the countenanced carbuncle—or Mashira—flooded with rage. "Oh, you're being such a pain!" he shouted, taking a step toward her. But, from the pit of his stomach, or quite literally from the middle of his abdomen, a gasp of astonishment escaped. The young man was getting up, perfectly healthy, devoid of a bullet hole or spattered gore. "You son of a bitch," the countenanced carbuncle said. Now he realized what the young man really was.

The world was bleached white. In the blink of an eye, streaks of light coming from nowhere in particular slammed head-on into the huntsman's abdomen. Flames rose from him, the stench of melting fat filled the air, and the huntsman fell into the brush with a thud.

It was almost as if the nerves that had endured this truly unearthly confrontation finally frayed and snapped—the girl started to fall like a puppet whose strings had been cut. Grove caught her gently.

When the figure that easily scooped up the girl had gone down the hill with her and out of sight, a low voice could be heard around the ankles of the still flaming corpse. "Well, spank my ass!" it said. "That's about what I'd expect from one of the Marcus clan. Now that I've seen his powers firsthand, I can't help wondering what the real *him* is like."

†

Leila had never seen the woman up close before. She didn't think her golden hair and creamy complexion were beautiful. She herself suited D better. But it was certain that behind those glamorous looks, the Barbarois woman possessed powers that staggered the imagination. Leila didn't take her lightly. Realizing in an instant that her javelin would be useless against this opponent, she jabbed it into the ground and drew the sliver gun.

Caroline pursed her lips and smiled. "Do you think you can defeat a woman from the village of the Barbarois with a toy like that?" she laughed. "I'll have you know, even the Nobility have no easy time getting into our village."

Instead of replying, Leila squeezed the sliver gun's trigger. Imperceptible needles pierced the woman's stomach without making a sound.

"Oh," Caroline cried, but soon enough she grinned broadly. "A gun that fires needles? You should've aimed for my heart, little girl."

Not knowing quite what she meant by that remark, Leila stood stock still with amazement. Suddenly, something fell from overhead and struck her right hand. The sliver gun went flying. Something speared down into the moss between the gun and the hand she stretched out to retrieve it, foiling her efforts. On discovering it was a thick tree branch, Leila leapt back, but something else caught hold of her by the shoulder. It was another branch, huge and bristling with countless twigs. Twisting the twigs with a crisp snap, the branch wrapped them around Leila's limbs like fingers.

"When I learned you'd arrived here ahead of me, I drank the sap of all the trees in the area," said Caroline. "Sap is the lifeblood of trees. So now, every one of their branches is mine—I have thousands of hands and feet."

"No, you can't be . . . " Goaded by a fearful foresight, Leila writhed, but she couldn't get free of the branches that were now her bonds.

"Ha ha, regrettably, I am not a Noble." Caroline wore the smile of a victor. "However, I have inherited some of their abilities. My mother, you see, was a wet-nurse for the Nobility overseeing Sector Seven of the Frontier."

Oh, it couldn't be that this gorgeous woman was a dhampir like D. Inhumanly beautiful. Mysteriously refusing to dine. Throwing feverish glances at Mayerling—hadn't all of these things indicated the woman's true nature? Even the way she could move about in daylight without difficulty fit the pattern.

However, her powers proved that she was indeed one of the Barbarois. Whatever felt her fangs—even inorganic things like the mechanical arm, or non-sentient lifeforms like the vegetation that bound Leila—obeyed her in the same way that humans followed the will of the Nobles who bit them. While most dhampirs would drink blood, they didn't convert anyone, so her ability was truly fearsome in comparison.

Looking from D to Leila and back again, Caroline let an evil little grin escape. "From what I saw just now, I'd say you're in love with that dhampir. How interesting. I was going to make short work of you, but I've changed my mind. I want you to watch as I go over there and skewer the heart of the man you love. And after that, I'll let you share his fate."

"Don't," said Leila. "If you're gonna kill anyone, kill me—"

"How courageous," Caroline replied with a laugh. "It seems even human scum who make their livelihood murdering the Nobility are far more tolerant when it comes to someone they adore. Well, just wait. You'll follow after him soon enough . . . " Caroline stated sternly, but as she did so an unbelievably chill breeze stroked her back. This female dhampir, possessing powers comparable to D's, turned around despite herself.

There was no change in the way D lay. What could that gorgeous man be dreaming of? Of the ordinary life that he, as a dhampir, could never know? Of days long passed? No, no, of a future painted in blood and pitch-black, with battles that would know no end—of that there could be no doubt.

"Just my imagination?" Caroline muttered as she raised her right hand. A branch from one of the massive trees around her bent at the trunk and pointed its trenchant tip at the Barbarois woman's chest. Grabbing it in her pale hand, Caroline snapped the branch off a yard back from the tip.

Slowly, she went to the side of the sleeping D and placed her feet so they straddled the depression. With both hands, she took a firm grip of the branch—the gigantic stake she'd improvised—and the instant she was about to swing it down from over her head . . .

Leila's scream of "Stop!" and her own strike were almost simultaneous, and it was in the next instant that Caroline cried out "Mashira?!"

The stake was caught in midair. By D's left hand. By the palm of his left hand, to be precise. And, as might be expected from Caroline's puzzled cry, what stopped the keen point was indeed the tiny mouth that appeared in the palm of his hand. The stake had literally been stopped by the skin of those teeth. Above the mouth, a pair of mischievous eyes laughed. And yet, his jaws were so powerful that even Caroline with her superhuman strength couldn't make them budge in the least. Her beautiful visage distorted by surprise and horror, the female dhampir leapt away.

"I'll thank you not to be calling me by strange names," the face in the palm said, effortlessly spitting the stake out of the depression.

"That Mashira—he's one of your cohorts? He's one of my kind then, I take it?"

Without answering, Caroline made a sweep of her right hand. The forest shook. Several gigantic trees bent and swung their branches straight down at the sleeping dhampir.

The left hand countered with an attack of his own. Grabbing hold of the huge branch it'd just spat out, it hurled the wooden missile at Caroline. The branch went with such speed there was no time to dodge it. And yet, Caroline must've managed at least a lightning-fast twist of her body, because it was her abdomen that the huge branch ultimately pierced.

The instant she fell backward screaming, the movements of the branches came to a dead stop. Even Leila's bonds came undone.

Seeing that she didn't even have time to make a dash for her javelin, Leila ran at Caroline. Latching onto the branch impaling the female dhampir, Leila shoved with all her might. Blood bubbled from Caroline's mouth.

"You little bitch you!" the female dhampir screamed. Her whole body twitching in the throes of death, her pale hands seized Leila's shoulders.

Leila didn't stop pushing, even when the blood-rimmed mouth clamped onto her neck. The only thing in her mind was, *I've gotta save D*, and that thought alone.

The mouth quickly fell away. An intense feeling of relaxation swept over Leila, and she allowed the huge branch to be snatched from her grasp.

Backing away a few steps, Caroline groaned again. The huge branch still pierced her abdomen, and from the waist down she'd been dyed crimson by the blood gushing from her. It was a sight nothing could rival.

"Little girl, we shall meet again. And next time, you will be my slave." Blood mixing with the words she spouted, Caroline turned and left.

Leila went to her knees on the ground. She'd just been bitten. Bitten by a dhampir. She felt no wonder, no fear. Only fatigue and a feeling of satisfaction. She'd kept her promise. The promise she'd made to herself. Still, Leila managed to pick herself up and go over to the sleeping D. Gazing down at his beautiful face for a long time, she said goodbye. "I wanted to kiss you," she said, "but I can't now. I mean, you'd wind up a laughing stock if some reject vampire were to steal a kiss from a Hunter like you. So long. If you can, try to think of me from time to time."

Barely managing to take the sliver gun and javelin in hand, Leila walked away. Her tottering figure was soon swallowed by the forest.

But how long would D continue to sleep? After all, the warrior woman who'd risked her life and soul defending him was wounded, Mayerling's lady love had run off somewhere, and the situation was only growing more confused . . .

III

The scene was the road, about two hours after Caroline and Leila's deadly battle had ended. Knifing its way through the wind at a speed of twenty-five miles per hour, the bus came to a sudden stop when something was spotted up ahead.

"What is it?" Borgoff called out in a gruff voice from where he was prepping his bow and arrows in his bedroom.

"A woman just crossed the road dead ahead of us. A blonde in a blue dress—probably that Caroline character Grove mentioned. I'm gonna go have a little look-see." As he spoke, Kyle got to his feet with the crescent blades in hand.

"Wait up—I'll go with you."

In reply to Borgoff's offer, he said, "Don't sweat it. It's just a woman. Besides, what if someone's trying to lure us both outside so they can take out Grove while we're gone? There's another one of them somewhere, you know."

"You've got a point there," Borgoff conceded. "Be careful."

"Hey, just leave it to me."

Smiling with overwhelming self-confidence, Kyle got off the bus. Although noon had already come and gone, the sunlight was hot and white. With crescent blades in either hand, as he was about to enter the woods in the same spot where the woman had vanished, he said, "Just to be on the safe side," and let the blades fly.

There couldn't have been any stranger ranged weapon than Kyle's crescent blades. Controlled with the fingertips of the hand that held one end of the thin wire, the semicircular blades attached to the other end of each line swept easily between the densely overlapping trees and came back to Kyle's hands. If his foe was lurking anywhere within a hundred-foot radius of the entrance to the forest, fresh blood drawn from her head or throat should've remained on the edge of his crescent blades at the very least. Better yet, she might even be dead already.

"Looks like no contact," Kyle said to himself. He went into the woods. Casually taking a few steps, he shouted, "There you are!"

A silvery flash coursed to the base of a gigantic tree, and, just when it seemed it would strike the trunk, it suddenly turned and shot straight upwards.

Caroline screamed and fell to the ground. Not the slightest trace remained of where she'd been staked with a huge branch two hours earlier, but now she held her exposed and bloody thigh and moaned. The crescent blade had slashed it open.

"What do you wanna do, Barbarois bodyguard?" Kyle snickered cruelly. "Don't be shy. Take your best shot, if you're game." While Kyle snorted that she wasn't all she was cracked up to be and extended both his arms for the *coup de grace*, his eyes were blasted by the woman's orbs. There was an indescribable light in her eyes.

Without time to realize how bad this development was, Kyle went and knelt by the woman's side. Her exposed thigh was burned into his retinas.

"Are you okay?" His consciousness drifting in a dream, Kyle heard himself ask a question that wasn't even in his mind.

"I think I'll be fine," the woman practically moaned. "My leg hurts. I really must stop the bleeding—would you be so kind as to lick it clean?"

The fact that this woman was a Barbarois sorceress no longer concerned Kyle. "Sure . . . no problem," he sort of mumbled, then put his mouth to her bare, white leg. His lips were instantly sullied with blood. Licking the outside clean, when he worked his way to her inner thigh, the woman began panting in earnest and wrapped her other leg around Kyle's waist. Kyle's blood-tinted lips pressed in even further.

When the moans of pleasure and lapping sounds had stopped, the woman gently put her hands on Kyle's cheeks. Her unblemished white face approached the blood-stained visage he raised at her bidding. Kyle had no comprehension how fearful the woman's actions had become.

And yet, while his instincts may have guessed the danger he was in, the fingers that reached with exasperating slowness for the crescent blade at his waist were caught by one of the woman's gentle hands.

"Oh no you don't," she chided. "You can use those to serve me once I'm done kissing you . . . " Her voice alone rang in his head, and, before long, the blackest darkness suffused his mind through her lips.

When Kyle came out of the forest a short time later, he raised his hand up over his head to shield his eyes from the sun. Slowly, he returned to the bus.

Borgoff was in the driver's seat. "How did it go?" he asked.

"She wasn't in there. Looks like she got away, but you can't be too careful."

"Hmm. Trade places with me," said the oldest Marcus. Standing to let Kyle take the driver's seat, Borgoff returned to the bedroom. Kyle was holding the wheel mutely. "Say, Kyle . . . "

Borgoff called out to him. Kyle didn't move. Borgoff called his name again.

"Er—What?" Kyle responded, his tone distant and removed.

"I'll let you in on a little shortcut. Pretty soon, we'll come to a spot where there's a red branch sticking out on our left. Turn in there. Once we're on that road, just follow it straight and we'll come out near the Claybourne States."

"Gotcha," Kyle replied.

The vehicle went a bit, then stopped.

"What happened?" asked Borgoff.

"The engine stalled. Looks like the oil charger is all screwed up. Give me a hand fixing it."

Empty-handed, Borgoff followed Kyle off the bus.

"Hold on a sec. I'll scout around first," said Kyle, moving to the front of the vehicle and out of Borgoff's line of sight. Borgoff scanned their surroundings and gave a light scratch to his head. And, having scratched, he leapt.

A bewitching light zipped out of the gap between the vehicle's undercarriage and the ground. As Borgoff looked askance at the pair of crescent blades sparking together in the spot where he'd stood, his right hand went into action. Grabbing the bow and arrows tucked through the back of his belt, he readied them in midair. There was a sound like the plucking of a zither's strings as he loosed two arrows simultaneously. What was really strange about the shot was how his arrows hit the tangled crescent blades, turned a few times, and slid up along the wires attached to the blades.

A low groan could be heard from the far side of the bus.

Borgoff circled around the vehicle to stand over the fallen Kyle. One steel arrow quivered in his brother's stomach and another was stuck through the top of his head. "I didn't want to have to do this to my own brother, but I didn't really have a choice," he told Kyle. "You went and got turned by a vampire. But at least now I know what she really is. I'll avenge you, so rest easy." Notching a third arrow, Borgoff took aim at his agonized brother's heart. "The next time you're reborn as a vampire, try not to shade your eyes from the sun when it's not all that bright out." And he watched until the bitter end, until the steel shaft had pierced his younger brother's heart.

A Port to the Stars

CHAPTER 6

I

H e was at a bit of a loss. On account of the girl. He wasn't entirely sure what he should do with her. Though the girl was as vibrant as a sunny day, she hadn't said anything about where she lived or why that huntsman with the countenanced carbuncle was chasing her. Of course, in this form Grove couldn't very well ask her, so he had no choice but to wait for her to tell him about it. When the girl had regained consciousness, she'd tried to go into the forest right away. Grove made a move to go with her, but she seemed troubled by that so he decided to stay out of it. But, on further consideration, it would be dangerous for a woman to be in the woods alone.

According to what the girl had said, she was going through the woods in a carriage with someone else when that huntsman attacked them, or something like that. Grove had his doubts that the story was as simple as that, because some parts of the girl's tale just didn't fit together right. He got the impression the fuzzier parts of her story were somehow connected to him and his brothers, but that didn't present a problem for him in his current state.

Seeing the girl off as she thanked him repeatedly and left, he started after her a few minutes after she'd vanished into the woods, but she hadn't gone more than a stone's throw from the entrance—

she was just standing there. Ultimately, he ended up going with her in search of her lover, just as she'd asked him to.

After an hour of walking around looking for the love of her life, the girl was nearly exhausted. She was breathing hard and beads of sweat were strung close together on her brow.

So weak, he thought, confident in his own healthy body. At that thought, he felt a swell of pity. He really wanted to help her find whoever she was looking for. After all, there was no telling when he'd have to go back.

Getting the girl on her feet again, he was helping her continue the search when twilight came calling. The woods were dangerous at night. He tried to lead the girl out of the forest, but it didn't go very well. Now he was lost, too. When the girl saw him with his shrugged shoulders, Grove was afraid she might get scared, but to his great surprise she giggled. Whether she'd been traveling with her lover or not, she must've had guts to take a carriage ride this far off the beaten trail on the Frontier.

Though her brightness seemed to know no end, there was just a hint of melancholy in her smile that whipped up Grove's protective instincts. At this point, the girl said something rather odd—that as soon as it was night, her lover was sure to come looking for her. Dubious of her confidence-filled eyes, he couldn't believe that would be the case. They'd be better off asking his brothers—who should be getting closer by the minute—for help.

Circling around behind the girl so as not to startle her, Grove sent a bolt of lightning into the air. The white-hot streak stretched up into the deepening blue of the evening sky without a sound.

†

Borgoff was in the driver's seat of the bus coming out of a cramped valley, and his narrow eyes sparkled at the sight of the energy bolt. "Wow, if ol' Grove has gone to all the trouble of giving us a signal—Well, he must've found something."

†

Dashing through woods sealed in darkness, Caroline glanced up at the heavens and grinned broadly. "That's the same light I saw back in the village," she said. "Surely it's a signal that boy has found something."

†

Deep in thought as he bent over the corpse of what had been Mashira, Mayerling snapped to attention at the heaven-splitting bolt of light rising from a part of the woods not so far away. "I was wondering who might've slain Mashira," he muttered, "Such raw power . . . Well, I don't care who it is. If they've laid a hand on that young lady, it won't be pretty, by my oath."

†

The girl felt oddly at peace. That was thanks to the youth in front of her. His innocent face and baby-soft complexion gave her an unrivaled sense of security. The young man didn't seem to fit into the forests of Frontier, but seemed like he'd be more suited for a life in the Capital.

The sun would be setting soon. Her love would probably be here in no time. No matter where she might be, she knew he'd find her. The girl was positive of that. As she played her gentle gaze over the youth standing before her in the caress of the evening breeze, the girl thought how sad how it was that he looked so healthy and yet couldn't speak a word.

Suddenly, the girl blinked. The young man turned her way, seeming surprised. A grove of trees was visible through his bright face. The youth was fading away.

His sad eyes gazed at the girl, and his lips formed a word. *Goodbye.*

The girl reached out to him. The youth was growing ever more transparent, like glass disappearing in water. *Goodbye*, the girl said frantically. Regardless of who he really was, she wanted to thank him as he left. *Goodbye, goodbye, thank you and goodbye.*

And then the youth vanished. In a corner of the woods growing darker and duskier, the girl was left alone.

The wind seemed to grow chillier. The eyes of countless blood-crazed beasts peered out at her from the depths of the forest.

I'm scared, the girl thought from the very depths of her soul. *So scared. Hurry and save me, my love.*

There was a rustling of the tree branches. It came from somewhere behind her and off to the right. The girl spun around. Someone was approaching. She couldn't tell if it was a man or a woman, or how they were dressed. Fear wound tight around her throat. It was coming closer. The sound of moss being trampled and twigs snapping. Fifteen or twenty feet ahead of her, the figure stopped moving.

A probing voice asked, "Who's that over there? That you, Grove?"

Even though the girl knew it was a woman's voice, her fears hadn't dissipated. She remembered that the man who'd attacked her earlier had two partners, and one of them was female. As for the name of the other man, she couldn't recall it.

When the figure took a step forward and she could make out the face of a woman she'd never seen before, the girl finally gave a deep sigh and let the tension escape from her shoulders.

"Let me guess—Are you the passenger from the carriage?" Well suited to the black hue of the scarf wound about the base of her neck, the woman was none other than Leila Marcus.

"And you are . . . ?" The girl's face, which had filled with joy when it turned out the new arrival wasn't Caroline, grew tight as soon as she saw how Leila was outfitted. A javelin and a sliver gun— there could be no mistaking the trappings of a Hunter. There was no way a Hunter would just be hanging around a place like this alone. Which could only mean she'd come here after her. First Mashira, now a Hunter—with one terrifying encounter mounting on the next, the girl's shoulders fell despondently.

"I didn't get to see your face back there, but you're the girl that was in the black carriage, aren't you?" Leila said nonchalantly. "I'm Leila Marcus. I'm a Vampire Hunter here to get your boyfriend."

The girl braced a hand against the ground.

"What's wrong?" Leila asked incredulously. "You get to go home now."

Though she listened to the Marcus woman's words with suspicion, the girl wasn't focused enough to catch how Leila's voice seemed a little feeble. "Go. Please," she urged the Hunter. "Just hurry up and get out of here."

"I asked you what's the matter?"

"I'm sure my love will be here soon," the girl said. "The two of you will fight until one of you is dead. And I don't want to make either of you kill on my account."

Leila looked at the blue darkness steadily filling the vicinity. She nodded. "I suppose you're right. The night is the Nobility's world . . . " For an instant, the fierce expression of a warrior steeled for battle arose on her face, but it was soon replaced by one that was strangely filled with half-hearted hatred. And once again, this time in a surprised manner, she asked, "Are you . . . you're still human, aren't you?"

The girl nodded.

"So, the Noble didn't have his way with you and drag you off then. Seriously, you didn't go of your own free will . . . That's what happened, isn't it?!"

"Yes, I did," the girl said with a nod. The pale beauty gazed at Leila. There was a powerful light to her eyes. So long as they had that, a person could endure just about anything.

"So that's what happened . . . " A feeling of envy and sadness softened Leila's tone. "You love him, don't you? In love with a Noble."

The girl didn't answer her. Her silence was her answer. But her eyes were sparkling.

Leila leaned up against the trunk of the gigantic tree. At her core was this hot stickiness. It was spreading through her whole body like a fog borne on the wind. It was fatigue. Twenty years worth of fatigue had finally seeped into her body.

Leila gazed at the girl. This girl had been carried off by a Noble and had given up being human, yet still had infinite confidence and trust. She, on the other hand, was renowned as one of the greatest Vampire Hunters on Earth but was now merely awaiting a horrid fate. Could it be that the pursued was happier than the pursuer?

"Doesn't it bother you?" Leila asked the girl.

"Huh?"

"Doesn't it bother you? Living on the run. He has no place to go back to, no tomorrow."

"Neither do I," the girl replied.

"Yeah, I suppose that would help the two of you get along."

The girl smiled thinly. "Never mind about me. Get out of here while you can. He'll be here soon."

"I don't care," said Leila. "I'm plumb exhausted. I'll wait here for your beloved. So, why don't we continue our little chat."

A low voice from behind them said, "I don't suppose you'd let yours truly listen in as well?"

The girl screamed, and Leila whipped around with ungodly speed. The face that greeted the eyes of both was that of the huntsman.

II

At the entrance to the same woods where he'd seen the streak of light, Borgoff stopped the vehicle. For a while, he didn't move from the driver's seat. A strange expression arose on his face when he got to his feet. An expression stripped of every emotion— almost the face of an imbecile.

Slipping through the sleeping quarters, Borgoff went into the arsenal and pulled a small timer and explosive from a wooden crate, then returned to the bunks. Going over to Groveck's bed, he carefully pulled away the blanket. An emaciated face appeared. He put his rough thumb to the barely colored lips. There was a faint flow of air. Groveck was still alive.

A single tear coursed from Borgoff's eye. When that shining bead snagged in his frightful beard, it hung there forever.

"It looks like it's down to just you and me," Borgoff said to the dearest of his brothers. It was this, the third born, that he loved more than Nolt or Kyle, or even more than Leila. "But this job's just about up to the big finale. I really need your power here. Which is all well and good, but you just got back from an attack and there's no reason you'd be having another one right away."

At this point, Borgoff sobbed. "That's why it's gotta be this way. I hate to say it, but you're gonna have to let me give you one. Looks to me like you ain't gonna stand but one more of these attacks. Once you have the next one, there'll be no saving you. That being the case, I want you to give your life for me."

His words could be taken as both sorrowful and unsettling, but what Borgoff did as he wept was horrific. Turning down the blanket even more, right about where his brother's heart was— over the thin sternum and above the jutting ribs—he taped the time bomb. Though the time bomb was just four inches of plastic tubing, the explosive packed in it would easily blow away the ribs and take out part of Grove's internal organs.

That couldn't possibly be what he planned to do to his brother's chest as Grove lay fighting for breath, could it?

Borgoff said he was sorry. His tears flowed without end.

Give your life for me.

While one strip of tape would've been enough to guard against the bomb slipping off, Borgoff put on a third layer, then a fourth, just in case Groveck tried to peel it off. Once he finished his work and had gently replaced the blanket, Borgoff lightly stroked his brother's forehead. "So long," he said. "I'll make it back for sure." And then, with his deadly bow and quiver of arrows across his back, he headed outside with an easy gait.

Evening was about to change from blue to black.

Borgoff ran. His gut told him from which way Groveck's streak of light had come.

His pace gradually quickened. The muscles in his legs creaked and popped as they swelled, and, perhaps more surprisingly, even the bones grew thicker. His upper body remained as massive as ever, but his lower limbs had been transformed into the legs of a veritable giant. And yet, his feet made almost no noise as they struck the mossy ground. In fact, they barely left a dent in the moss.

Perhaps this was a behest from his parents, who were said to have possessed genetic engineering technology. But why was it that when he walked up a slope, his body remained nearly perpendicular to the terrain?

He entered the woods. At a speed nearly five times that of an ordinary person, he headed deeper into the trees. The way his feet moved, it seemed like they didn't know the meaning of the word stop. Soon, however, they came to a sudden halt. He'd just run into a bizarre area. There he could see what looked like a model of the Capital made entirely out of dirt. A cluster of conical buildings roughly fifteen feet high were connected by transport tubes a foot and a half thick. The Capital seemed to run on forever into the forest.

However, Borgoff's gaze was not trained so much on the structures themselves as on the ground beneath his feet. There were white things scattered about—a skull staring fixedly at him with gaping black sockets, a femur that looked like it would make an improvised ax, ribs, a humerus . . . They were all bones. Most of them were from species Borgoff recognized, the rest were from birds and beasts he wasn't familiar with, but the human bones were certainly easy enough to spot. Despite all the remains, the air here didn't have the slightest stench of decay. It was as if something had stripped them of their flesh and blood.

Leaving only his startled exclamation of "Whoa!" in his old position, Borgoff jumped forward a good six feet. He landed without disturbing the moss. At the spot he'd just leapt away from, there were a number of creatures that looked like black grains of rice scurrying around. "Sorry, I can't afford to be dinner for you guys just yet," he called back to the minute creatures. "So long." There was something horrifying about his voice as he spoke, and then, when he was about to make another bound, a shudder ran down his spine. In that instant, he realized who he was going to be up against. The distance to the foe he sensed was twenty-five feet ahead and a little to the right, with the eerie model of the Capital lying dead in the middle.

All the power drained from Borgoff's body. Preparing for battle, he struck a pose that would let him use his muscles just as he wanted. The tension others might feel when a fight to the death was imminent meant nothing to a Hunter of Borgoff's class. Crouching to escape the fierce, unearthly aura shooting through him, Borgoff let an arrow fly with lightning speed. He already had another arrow cocked and ready.

The unearthly aura died out.

The Hunter didn't know where his arrow had gone or what effect it had. But from the way there was no sound of leaves or twigs swaying, he could well imagine.

The air stirred by his right cheek. He jumped forward for all he was worth. What had just split the air and then stuck itself into the ground was the arrow he'd fired. While the fact that someone had stopped his shot with their bare hands didn't surprise him, the awesome power with which it'd been hurled back gave Borgoff goosebumps. Any stone or branch out there might become a deadly weapon in the hands of his enemy.

Up ahead of him, the Hunter sensed someone moving. Picking himself up and preparing to loose a second arrow, Borgoff stiffened. There against the backdrop of blue darkness, a figure in black suddenly stood. Borgoff's Hunter-sharp eyes caught the pair of fangs poking out from the corners of his foe's proper mouth.

"So you're my prey then? We meet at long last," Borgoff said in a tone brimming with delight as he aligned the neck of his deadly arrow with his foe's heart.

"I have no words of greeting for a stray dog out prowling for human flesh and blood," the figure garbed in black said quietly. "However, I have no desire for needless conflict. If you put your tail between your legs and scamper off, I won't do anything to you."

Borgoff laughed. "That's kind of you to offer." The direction his arrow was aiming was gradually changing. Towards the sky. "But I'm afraid I can't!"

What Borgoff did next was nearly miraculous. At almost exactly the same time as the two arrows he shot vertically left his bowstring, he took two more from his quiver and launched them at his target. The speed of his attack was so great, the Noble—Mayerling—was clearly shaken. Another shaft flew through the air as if to block Mayerling's way after he barely blocked the first two and moved to the right. The Noble had to twist in midair to avoid it. The instant he landed, two more arrows thunked into the ground at his feet in rapid succession.

Mayerling leapt backward. A shout of rage split his lips. How could a mere mortal with no more than a primitive bow and arrow put him in such peril?!

However, one last surprise remained in the trap Borgoff had laid. When Mayerling tried to twist out of the way of the whining menace dropping from above, his eyes caught sight of a black light knifing though the darkness. No matter where he leapt, he'd be under fire! And, when his movements stiffened for an instant, two arrows dropped out of the sky on an almost perfectly vertical path and pierced both of the Noble's shoulders with what seemed like calculated precision.

Groaning in agony, Mayerling went to pull the arrows out, but his hands wouldn't move.

"It's no use," Borgoff chortled. "I don't care if you're a Noble or not, you ain't gonna be able to pull them out. For starters, you can't raise your arms. So, how do you like my chaser arrows bit?"

Borgoff's confidence-choked laughter was certainly fitting praise for his own masterful skill. Taking into account where the first two arrows he fired would drop, he'd driven Mayerling there with his relentless waves of attacks. However, Mayerling had been free to move as he liked. What could possibly rope in someone with several times the speed and strength of a human, and herd him right into the target in the instant the arrows fell? Borgoff's ungodly skill—and the chaser arrows—could.

At that moment, something about the scene changed. The ground at Mayerling's feet suddenly had a blackness to it. Something like an inky stain was surging forward, headed in his direction. When he tried to jump out of the way, callous steel whistled past him on either side.

Shrilly, Borgoff asked, "Well, what's wrong? Aren't you gonna run away? Can't escape now, can you? If you move, I'll put an arrow through your heart. Of course, them mints have caught the smell the blood, and if you stand there you'll be their next meal."

He was right. The wave of black steadily approaching Mayerling's feet was in fact a large swarm of fearsome flesh-eating ants, otherwise known as mints. This spot so reminiscent of the Capital was indeed a metropolis—a cathedral for hundreds of millions of the smallest and fiercest of creatures.

"Well, well, well. You don't have time to think it over," said Borgoff. "What'll it be—one right through the heart, or are you gonna wind up in the belly of them mints with nothing but your bones left behind? Nobility or not, you can't come back from just bones. What'll it be?"

When Borgoff had slowly pulled his bowstring taut, he saw the Noble's hands go into motion.

†

Who the hell are you?" asked Leila. The man didn't look like someone she'd need anything as heavy as the sliver gun against, and she held her javelin casually as she stood in front of the huntsman. It was only when Leila caught sight of the charring on Mashira's stomach that her face hardened. *I'd swear that's a wound from one of Groveck's power rays,* she thought. *And yet, this guy's still—*

"That's not him," the girl cried out in a quavering voice. "Originally, he was one of our bodyguards. But he transferred himself into a different body. He's got this other face on his stomach that—" Before she could finish, the girl doubled over like a shrimp, as if victim to agonizing stomach pains.

Unsure what was happening, Leila let the javelin fly. Her "shoot first, ask questions later," Hunter habits had come to the fore. The man didn't move. The javelin should've sunk into his stomach, but, when the tip of it was stopped by a sharp clang, Leila leapt back. As she leapt, her right hand grabbed hold of the sliver gun at her hip. The handle of the weapon shooting back out of the man's stomach knocked the gun out of her hand.

"Knock it off already," the man said. Apparently he could manipulate the nerves and vocal cords of a corpse, and this threatening outburst from the mouth of the deceased huntsman coupled with the raised barrel of the high-caliber rifle rooted Leila to the spot. "It's been a good while since I ran across a scrappy little hellcat like you," the huntsman said in the countenanced carbuncle's voice. "That's just perfect. I'll make both of you my women. Come on."

As if beckoned by that evil voice, Leila took a few steps forward. The huntsman's free hand lifted his shirt. Seeing the human face that swelled up on his belly, Leila cried out in surprise. Its lips pursed, and a terrifying brown ligament shot out at Leila's stomach.

A scream arose. It belonged to neither Leila, nor the girl. It'd been loosed by the countenanced carbuncle. There was a single needle of rough wood stuck right through the middle of the brown umbilicus the countenanced carbuncle apparently used to transfer itself. When the pain-wracked huntsman spun around in search of his foe, more needles pierced him through the heart and right between the eyes. Of course, the corpse didn't fall.

Though she didn't know exactly when he'd appeared, Leila launched an impassioned cry of "D!" at the rider and mount pausing in a shower of brilliant moonlight.

Watching as the dashing Vampire Hunter got off his horse, the huntsman didn't move.

"D, that's really . . . "

Nodding faintly at Leila's words, D reached back over his shoulder with his right hand. He hadn't let the countenanced carbuncle get away. The needle sticking through the transfer membrane also prevented it from sinking back into its body.

When the whine of a blade leaving its sheath rose from D's back, the huntsman's stomach suddenly bulged. With a *splat* like a stone thrown into a muddy ditch, a gray mass flew from the huntsman's abdomen. Blood and viscera streamed after it. The mass disappeared into the bushes with alarming speed.

"Oh, now this is a surprise," said a low voice issuing from around D's waist. "I didn't think any of my kind could fly through the air. What fun, what fun!"

Sheathing his naked steel, D didn't say a word as he walked toward Leila and the girl. Recovering from the sunlight syndrome took days, and, usually, the tougher a dhampir was, the longer it took for him to recuperate. But D already seemed to be over it, and the eyes he trained on the two young ladies swam with an impossibly black spirit. Perhaps this youth was no average dhampir after all.

"Oh ho ho. It looks like both of you are safe. You ought to thank me for spotting that light. Pretty boy here was still snoozing at the time." The faint voice from the Hunter's hand didn't reach the ears of Leila or the girl.

Following D's line of sight when she realized it wasn't on herself, Leila saw that the girl was slumped on the ground. She ran over in a panic. "C'mon, snap out of it!" she shouted.

D came over and bent down by the girl's side. Laying his left hand on top of the hands she had pressed against her own solar plexus, he asked, "Is it that *thing* we just saw?"

"Yep." At the answer emitted by his left hand, Leila's eyes went wide. "There's still time to save her if you do it now," the voice added.

D nodded. He lay the girl flat out on her back in the undergrowth, and gently placed her hands back down by her sides. His gorgeous hands went into action, exposing the girl's stomach.

Leila stifled a scream. In the center of that smooth, porcelain stomach, an ugly human face was rising to the surface. Its features were exactly the same as the one that'd been attached to the belly of the huntsman just moments earlier.

"All his little pals look the same," D's left hand stated. "What's more, they've got a collective consciousness. The thoughts of one are immediately transmitted to the others. These things can be a real pain in the ass."

"Why would it infect her?" asked D.

"Out of lechery, pure lechery. These critters have an appreciation for beauty and the finer things. On top of that, the dirty little bastards enjoy sex through the senses of the humans they inhabit. I imagine that's what he wanted to use her body for."

A naked blade glittered in D's right hand.

Perhaps realizing what D intended to do, the startled face was about to magically sink back into the girl. But the blade D thrust at its forehead lanced down into the oral cavity of the countenanced carbuncle with matchless precision. Screaming in anguish, it rolled its eyes back in their sockets. Streams of blood erupted from either side of its mouth before it started to fade back into the girl's body.

"That should do it! Now I guess it'll just be assimilated by her normal organs," said the voice.

Whether the procedure had been painful or not was unclear, but the girl had fainted. D stood up.

"What's the story with your left hand, D?" asked Leila.

D only replied, "You were bitten by that woman, weren't you?"

Leila nodded, her expression gloomy.

"Then that's someone else I have to put down."

"Huh?" Leila said with surprise.

"I repay my debts." D replied succinctly. He knew about the deadly struggle Leila had joined.

†

When the Noble's hand reached not for the corresponding shoulder but for the opposite armpit, Borgoff grew pale. Forgetting to fire his next deadly shot, he watched the impossible happen.

Getting a tight grip on the arrowhead sticking through his armpit, the Noble pulled it right out with one yank. Not up, but down. The other end, of course, was fletched with vanes to make it fly straight. Just like the shafts and heads of all Borgoff's arrows, the vanes were made of steel. Gouging flesh and shaving bone, the vanes went in the one direction that'd give the Noble his freedom again—they were pulled *down*. The Noble's actions and his supernatural strength flew in the face of logic.

Now he'll go for the other arrow . . . But just as Borgoff was thinking that, something whizzed through the air. The arrow the Noble had just removed.

An acute pain seared through Borgoff's abdomen. The arrow his foe had just thrown back at him had been going faster than those Borgoff shot. Borgoff stared dumbfounded at the end of the arrow that went in through his belly and jutted out his back. Blood traveled down the shaft in dribs and drabs. He heard the Noble address him.

"Our duel is over, stray mongrel. It shall be *you* that the mints feast on."

Borgoff opened his eyes wide. "I'm afraid not. This fight is just getting started."

Saying that, the Hunter ran. Right to the mint nest. The nest of the flesh-eating ants was little more than a fragile metropolis of soil hardened by an adhesive the ants themselves secreted. A large bird landing on it would be more than enough to crush it—to say nothing of what the weight of a grown man would do to it.

But Borgoff stood on the ant nest. Or rather, he stuck to it. Both his legs were at a right angle to the wall. What's more, he must've been using some sort of trick, because the fragile tower didn't show a single crack.

In that outré pose—which, not surprisingly, drew a cry of astonishment from Mayerling—Borgoff let his arrows fly. They no longer had the same power they'd had a few moments earlier. Mayerling's right hand went into action, and the murderous steel implements were struck down one after another.

Confusing his foe by moving over to one of the passageways and hanging upside down from it like a monkey, the Hunter dipped once more into his quiver. Suddenly, a strange sensation came from his legs. His profuse bleeding had robbed his legs of the ability to render him weightless, and he fell with the crumbling dirt into the very heart of the flesh-eating ants' nest.

His next sensation was that of countless insects swarming all over his body.

Borgoff screamed. Squeezing every last bit of power from his body, he got up and ran. Each footfall crushed towers, destroyed passageways—he didn't even feel the pain in his belly now. The fear of being eaten alive had his heart in its talons.

Deep into the woods he ran, his screams resounding through the trees.

III

The moonlight limned three faint shadows on the ground. D, Leila, and the girl.

Leila let out a deep sigh. The girl had just finished telling them the circumstances that'd brought her there. Only the wind moved near the trio, and darkness had fallen around them.

"There's just one thing I want to ask you," D said. He was still admiring the moonlight. "Are you aware that the Claybourne States are now . . . "

The girl nodded.

"I see," said D. "Then I guess you may as well go. But what'll you do then?"

"I don't know," the girl replied. "Once we get there, our journey will be over. One way or another."

D fell silent. The wind was singing a sad tune in the treetops.

"But it's something good," Leila muttered. "Love's so great . . . So why does it have to go so wrong?"

For a long time, none of the trio moved.

D made the moonlight sway. "It seems he's come for you," he said. His eyes indicated the depths of the forest.

Tears glistened in the girl's eyes. "Don't do this, I beg of you. Please, just let me go to him. If we keep going at this rate, we'll reach the Claybourne States by tomorrow night. Everything will end there. After that . . . "

D faced the forest.

"Don't move," Leila said. D turned to face her. She had the barrel of the sliver gun aimed at his chest. "Let her go. We can settle things once they reach the Claybourne States."

D didn't move.

"Thank you," said the girl. "Thank you—thank you both."

In the depths of the woods, a tall silhouette hove into view. The girl ran to it. Pausing for an instant, the two silhouettes vanished among the trees as if embraced by the forest. Once they were gone, Leila lowered the sliver gun. "Sorry, D," she said.

"Why the apology? I should thank you again."

Leila said with surprise, "You don't mean you would've—"

"Go to sleep already. Tomorrow morning I'll take you to where to left your car. There we part company. After that, you can tail me, go back to your brothers, or whatever you like. You can count on me to take care of the female dhampir."

"I . . . " Leila swallowed the rest of the words. She was going to say she wanted to go with him. But how would she go about traveling with a shadow?

A blanket was tossed at her feet. D took another one in hand and walked over to the trunk of a nearby tree. Spreading the blanket on the ground, he sat back against the tree trunk and crossed his arms. The sword off his back had been placed by his left side.

After a moment's consideration, Leila sat down next to D. D gazed at her steadily. His pupils seemed deep enough to swallow her. Suppressing a wave of rapture, she asked, "Does this bother you? You know, where I'm a vampire victim and all?"

"Nope."

"Thanks," she said. Pulling the blanket up to her chest, Leila lay down on the ground, using her arm for a pillow.

There was a fragrance to the wind. Night-blooming jasmine, moonlit grass, nocturnal peonies, moonshine . . . Sweet and heart-rending . . . There was life by night. The croaking of frogs, music from the jaws of longhorns, the whispering of great silkworms . . . All small and tough and full of life . . .

For a moment, Leila forgot she was the prey of a female dhampir. It'd never been like this for her. "Funny, isn't it," she said as she scratched the tip of her nose.

D didn't move, but he seemed to be listening.

"The night doesn't frighten me a bit. None of my brothers has ever done this . . . Every single night, we had the feeling there were beasts and evil spirits out to get us . . . Even inside the bus, we were still on edge." And yet, now she seemed perfectly fine. "I wonder why I don't mind the night now?"

After she'd said it, Leila was surprised. Had she actually thought that stern young man would give her an answer? She said it herself, quietly, in her heart. *Because I'm with you . . .*

Even after Leila fell asleep listening to the song of the wind, the young Vampire Hunter still trained his gaze patiently on the darkness of the night, anger and grief far from the void that was his eyes.

†

At about the same time, in a part of the forest not very far away, a strange and truly disturbing event was unfolding.

Borgoff could feel his internal organs being bored through and devoured. There was no longer any pain. Ants were swarming all over his body. They were inside his face, too. He saw his right eye fall out. The sensation of ants crawling around in his eye socket was strangely tickling. Tens of thousands of them were dining on his flesh. Each and every trifling bite splashed a chill over him. It was cold. So very cold.

A strange thing clawed its way out of the grass and came into view of the corner of his remaining left eye. It was a gooey gray lump. Oddly enough, though it lacked arms and legs, it clearly had eyes and a nose.

"Oh, this is a nice little find I've made," said the lump. "It's a little beat up, but if I knock all the freaking ants off it I should be able to get some use out of it. Yessir, when it comes to traveling, you can't beat a human body." Moving over to Borgoff's mouth, it said to him, "You'll have to excuse me. I'm kind of in a hurry, too."

The gooey limbless lump pried open lips that the man himself lacked the strength to open, and Borgoff felt the thing sliding down his esophagus and into his stomach.

IV

There wasn't really any place called the Claybourne States any longer. Neighboring sectors had only heard about the Ninety-Eighth Frontier Sector's capital region because the spaceport was there, and the Claybourne States had come to be known by the spaceport's name as well. But that name, too, had long since been forgotten, and people hadn't mentioned either in ages.

With its automated housekeeping-systems destroyed, the interior of the terminal building was left to the rampant dust, and the winds that blew in through shattered panes of reinforced glass traced thin, swirling patterns in the accumulated grit.

A drifter who was calling one of the spaceport rooms his home that particular evening found his meager dinner interrupted by the untimely arrival of guests. A black carriage drawn by a half-dozen horses came in through the central gate. Once it halted at the entrance to the terminal building, two passengers got out. There was a man and a woman. What astonished the drifter was the fact that the couple consisted of a Noble and a human. Both of them went into the building, but the way they held each other's hands only added to his consternation. *A human and a Noble?* he thought to himself. *It couldn't be!* He slipped quietly out of his room and headed out of the spaceport as if he'd just had a nightmare.

†

The pair stood dazed in the blue dusk of the lobby. Or, to be more precise, only Mayerling was dazed. The pity in the girl's expression was directed at her love.

"No . . . This can't be . . . " Mayerling mumbled. His words echoed through the emptiness.

The only ships for sailing to the stars visible in the vast complex were horrible derelicts. A photon-powered spaceship with melted engines, a galaxy ship crushed in the middle, a dimension-warping schooner wrecked beyond repair . . . It was a quiet and cruel death that covered the apron. There was no road out there that might carry them together on a voyage among the stars.

"It can't be . . . " Mayerling stammered. "The rumors said . . . " In his mind, rumors that the spaceport still operated on a small scale must've seemed more and more real with each passing day, taking shape and becoming the absolute truth to him. Knowing his kind was doomed, even declaring as much himself, he remained a Noble after all.

As he stood paralyzed, a hand gently pressed upon his shoulder. He saw the girl's face. Her perfectly placid expression.

"It doesn't matter," she said. "We'll go somewhere else now. So long as I'm with you, I'll go anywhere. Together forever . . . until death do us part . . . "

"But—I can't die," Mayerling replied.

Tears welling in her eyes as they clung to him, the girl said in a determined tone, "In that case, make me just like you . . . "

"I can't do that."

"I don't mind." The girl shook her head. "I don't mind at all. I was prepared for that from the very start . . . "

Blue light tinged the faces of the young couple. Mayerling's face slowly approached the nape of the girl's neck. The girl had her eyes shut. Her long, lovely eyelashes trembled. When she felt the lips of her beloved on the base on her neck, her eyes snapped open.

A scream echoed through the lobby.

Mayerling stared in amazement at his love, who'd pulled free of him with that scream.

The girl's violent emotions quickly passed. A tremendous feeling of remorse showed on her face. Her lips quivered. "I . . . I . . . That was a horrible thing for me to do . . . " she stammered.

Mayerling smiled. It was the smile of a man who'd just lost something. "It's okay," he said gently. "We're fine the way we are. If you should wither and die first, I shall follow after you."

The girl crushed herself against him and hung on for dear life. She said not a word, but he softly stroked her quivering shoulders.

"Shall we go then?" he suggested. "Though the pathway to the stars is barred to us, we may yet journey across the earth."

The girl looked up at him and nodded. Stroking her waist-long hair in sympathy, he let his eyes wander to the lobby's exit. A figure in a black coat suddenly stood there. The blue pendant at his breast and his unsettling beauty burned into the Noble's retinas. Holding his tongue, Mayerling pushed the girl aside.

"Your trip's over," D said. "Give me the girl."

"Take her then. That is, if you survive," Mayerling said gruffly. He made no effort to keep his ladylove by his side and avoid the fight.

"This way, if you don't mind," Leila said to the girl as she came over from one of the other walls, took the girl by the hand, and brought her to the corner of the room.

D walked toward Mayerling. He stopped with ten feet still between them.

"You know, D," Mayerling said, discharging the words like a sigh, "there's no road to the stars after all. But then you knew that all along, didn't you?"

D didn't answer.

Vampire and Vampire Hunter discarded hatred and anger and grief, and readied for battle. Trenchant claws grew from the fingertips of Mayerling's right hand. Neither of the men seemed to move, but the distance between them shrank nonetheless.

A horizontal flash of black shot out, and D took to the air without a sound. The eldritch blade that howled with the Hunter's downward swipe hit Mayerling's left arm with a shower of sparks. Again the black claws swiped out in an attack, and again they met only air as D leapt back six feet.

This lobby, where nothing save ages of decay sat in stagnation, was playing host for this one night alone to a condensed conflict between life and death.

†

While her eyes were riveted to the pair's deadly battle, Leila felt warm breath brushing the nape of her neck. "Come this way," someone said to her. The voice was seductive and female. Oddly enough, the girl didn't seem to notice it at all. "Come this way," it said again.

Even when Leila quietly slipped to the rear, the girl and her soul remained prisoners of the deadly duel before them.

A knife of some sort was placed in Leila's right hand. "Take this and stab the girl," the voice told her. "Kill her!" The speaker must've still believed Mayerling would be hers if only she disposed of the girl.

Leila nodded. Her grip tightened on the handle of the knife. Circling around behind the girl, she stealthily raised the blade.

"Now!" the voice commanded.

Leila did a flip. Caroline's rapture-twisted face was right in front of her own now. Before the Barbarois woman's expression could register her shock, the silver knife was gouging deep into the female dhampir's heart. What's more, out of apparent concern about distracting the pair of combatants from their battle, Leila took the added measure of clamping her left hand down like a lid over Caroline's lips. Blood gushed out between Leila's fingertips.

As Caroline's eyes went from a look of agony and disbelief to a haze of death, Leila stared into them and smirked. "Too bad. You know, I noticed something while you were ordering me around. Seems there's at least one woman you bit who didn't wind up your own personal marionette." Leila, it seemed, possessed an unusual resistance to the demon's call, though she had not known it until now.

When Leila turned her eyes from the falling body of the beautiful woman, the death match seemed about to be decided.

As soon as he'd batted down all of the rough wooden needles D hurled at him during a leap back, Mayerling felt composure coming over his mind. It was the next instant that he saw a thick flash of silvery light. His injured arms hadn't recovered their previous speed yet. D's longsword, thrust with calculated precision at this hole in Mayerling's defenses, slid neatly into the Noble's stomach.

As the Noble thudded to the ground in a bloody mist, the girl ran like the wind to his side. "Please, try not to shake me so much," Mayerling told her. He smiled wryly under his pained breathing.

D came over. Two pairs of eyes met, the huntsman and the prey. Both men's eyes had a mysterious hue of emotion to them.

"You did well to dodge that strike," D said softly. No matter how deep the wound to Mayerling's stomach, it wouldn't be the end of a Noble. Once the sword was pulled out, even a wound from D would eventually heal.

"Why did you miss?" asked Mayerling.

The girl and Leila—who'd also come over once her own deadly little battle was done—looked at D in surprise.

Giving no answer, D bent over and took several strands of the girl's lengthy hair in hand. Pulling out a dagger, he cut off a lock about eight inches long and put it in one of his coat pockets. "So long as I have some of her hair, the sheriff's office will be able to confirm her identity," he said. "Baron Mayerling and his human love are dead. Never show yourselves before mankind again."

An indescribable light welled up in the girl's eyes.

D took hold of the hilt of his longsword and pulled the metal out of Mayerling's body. His blade rasped back into its sheath. "There's the ten million right there. Easy money." Without another word, D walked toward the exit.

"D!" Leila shouted. She was about to go after him, but at that moment a roaring wind caught her ear.

When D whipped around at the sound of flesh being penetrated, he saw the steel arrow that pierced Mayerling's chest. From the angle of it, he gleaned where it'd been fired from, and a flash of silvery white flew from D's right hand. It rebounded off the high ceiling and was barely blocked by a figure who made an easy, spider-like dash sideward.

"Borgoff!" Leila cried out.

D saw her brother, too. But was it really Borgoff? There was a huge, gaping hole in his stomach that did nothing to conceal the deep red scraps of entrails, sinew, and bone within. Half of either thigh was exposed bone, and the right side of his face was just a skull. Such was the fate one met when attacked by flesh-eating mint ants.

Laughing maniacally, he shouted, "You're next, jerk!"

Black bits of lightning streaked at D, but each and every one was struck down. The corpse didn't have quite the same skill it'd possessed in life. Hoping to attack from a different angle, Borgoff ran across the ceiling to the wall. He was confident of his speed. Of the speed he'd had in life.

A second later, his shoulder and the top of his head were pierced by flashes of white that shot vertically from below, where by all rights no one should've been able to get him. If that'd been the extent of the damage, the already dead Borgoff wouldn't have had any problems. Due to D's ungodly skill, however, one of the wooden needles rebounded and shattered his right ankle, which was just denuded bone. His remaining leg couldn't continue to support his weight of nearly two hundred and twenty-five pounds, and Borgoff's massive frame fell head over heels from a height of some thirty feet before smashing against the lobby floor.

"Damn it all!" He spat the words down at his own barely fleshed chest. "But if *his* memory serves me, there's still something I can do." Borgoff's grotesque right hand—bones with chunks of flesh still clinging to it—went into his pants pocket.

At that moment, the drifter who was searching for food in the bus parked right in front of the spaceport jumped as he heard a tiny explosion from one of the beds lined up in the back.

D was cloaked in a ghastly aura as he walked toward Borgoff, but, suddenly, a young man stood between them.

"There you are, Grove," Borgoff's corpse said in Borgoff's voice. "Do your thing! Kill all of these fuckers."

Before he'd finished speaking, D leapt. His longsword sank into the youth's shoulder and went through it like water.

The youth wasn't looking at D. He was gazing at the long-haired girl in a corner of the lobby as she cradled a figure in black and sobbed. A hue of sadness suddenly invaded his flushed face. He shook his head ever so slightly from side to side.

"Gro . . . Grove?!" Borgoff stammered in disbelief.

Before his brother had finished saying his name, the young man became transparent, then quickly faded away.

When agony seemed to force Grove's desiccated form to sit up in bed, the horrified drifter inched ever closer to him, but, the instant the youth appeared before him, the intruder was scared out of his mind. The youth's sad gaze was trained on the convulsing body, and then he put himself against it. The second he did, he started to melt into the feeble form, and a shudder ran through the still upright body. Then it moved no more.

Walking to Borgoff's body, D quickly pressed the palm of his left hand to its chest. There was an anguished cry. From Borgoff's feet.

Something squirming around inside Borgoff's thigh seemed to be gradually rising toward his chest, inch by inch, as if it was being pulled up on a string. Past the stomach it went, slipping through organs left exposed by the gaping wound, and when it reached the spot directly under the palm of D's hand, the crunch of meat and bone reverberated. It gave a scream in its death throes, but that ended soon enough.

D pulled his left hand away. The tiny mouth in the middle of his palm opened. From it, something like a catfish tail wriggled out, but it was soon sucked back in. Once again, there was the crunching sounds of mastication, and then its tongue lolled out to lick its lips before disappearing, lips and all.

Without even a glance at Borgoff, who was now a true corpse, D turned in the girl's direction. She'd fallen by Mayerling's side.

Checking her pulse, Leila looked at D and shook her tear-streaked face from side to side.

One of Mayerling's claws was jabbing into the girl's chest. The girl had taken hold of it and thrust it into her own bosom.

D's gaze was somewhat weary as he looked down at the amazingly serene countenance she wore in death. He heard Leila's voice from somewhere. *Love's so great . . . So why does it have to go so wrong?*

The human and the Noble—each died as they'd lived. The human as a human, the Noble as a Noble . . .

"She said thank you," Leila said absentmindedly.

D took the lock of hair out of his coat pocket. That was all that remained of the girl now.

Some time later, the drifter—who'd received a large sum in gold from the gorgeous young man in black to bury the pair—stepped into the lobby. The wind that slipped in with him blew the strands of hair from where they'd been placed on the girl's shoulder, scattering them randomly across the empty hall.

†

At the entrance to the spaceport, Leila got down off D's horse. "I'm going to this town up north," she said to the gorgeous countenance trained on her. "It's a little place, and it's always covered with snow, but this young guy who runs the butcher shop there asked me to marry him once. He's the only guy who ever knew my last name and said it didn't matter. By now, he's probably got a wife and kids already, but then he said he'd wait as long as he had to. I'm sorta counting on that."

D nodded. "Godspeed," he said.

"Right back at you."

D urged his horse forward. Leila remained stock still behind him, and about the time the blue darkness was starting to hide her, a faint smile slipped to D's lips. If Leila had caught sight of it, she probably would've reflected with pride on how her parting words had inspired it until the end of her days.

It was just such a smile.

And now, a preview of the next novel in the
Vampire Hunter D series

Vampire Hunter D

Volume 4
Tale of the Dead Town

Written by
Hideyuki Kikuchi

Illustrations by
Yoshitaka Amano

English translation by
Kevin Leahy

Now available
from Dark Horse Books and Digital Manga Publishing

Journey By Night

I

O n the Frontier, nothing was considered more dangerous
than a journey by night.

Claiming the night was their world, the Nobility had once
littered the globe with monsters and creatures of legend, as if to
adorn the pitch black with a touch of deadly beauty. Those same
repugnant creatures ran rampant in the land of darkness even
after the dominance of the Nobility had faded. That was how the
vampires bared their fangs at the way of the world, a human
idea that ordained the light of day as the time for action and the
dark of night for restfulness. The darkness of night was the greatest
of truths, the vampires claimed, and the ruler of the world. *Farewell,
white light of summer.*

That was why the night was filled with menace. The moans of
dream demons lingered in the wind, and the darkness whispered
the threats of dimension-ripping beasts. Just beyond the edge of the
woods glowed eyes the color of jasper. So many eyes. Even well-armed
troops sent into devastated sections of the Capital felt so much
relief after they'd slipped through the blocks of dilapidated
apartment complexes they'd flop down right there on the road.

Out on the Frontier it was even worse. On the main roads,
crude way-stations had been built at intervals between one lodging

place and the next. But, when the sun went down on one of the support roads linking the godforsaken villages, travelers were forced to defend themselves with nothing more than their own two hands and whatever weapons they could carry. That was why there were only two kinds who would actually choose to travel by night. The Nobility. And dhampirs. Particularly if the dhampir was a Vampire Hunter.

Scattering the shower of moonlight far and wide, the shadowy form of a horse and rider climbed a desolate hill. The mount was just an average cyborg horse, but the features of the rider were as clean and clear as a jewel, like the strange beauty of the darkness and the moon crystallized. Every time the all-too-insistent wind touched him, it trembled with uncertainty, whirled, and headed off bearing a whole new air. Carrying a disquieting aura. His wide-brimmed traveler's hat, the ink black cape and scarf darker than darkness, and the scabbard of the elegant longsword that adorned his back were all faded and worn enough to stir imaginings of the arduous times this traveler had seen.

The young traveler had his eyes closed, perhaps to avoid the wind-borne dust. His profile was so graceful it seemed the Master Craftsman in heaven above had made it His most exquisite work. The rider appeared to be thoroughly exhausted and immersed in a lonely sleep. Sleep—for him it was a mere break in the battle, but a far cry from peace of mind.

Something else mixed with the groaning of the wind. The traveler's eyes opened. A lurid light coursed into them, then quickly faded. His horse never broke its pace. A little over ten seconds was all they needed to reach the summit of the hill. Now the other sounds were clear. The crack of a gun and howls of wild beasts.

The traveler looked down at the plain below, spying a mid-sized motor home that was under attack. Several lesser dragons were prowling around it—more "children of the night" sown by the Nobility. Ordinarily, their kind dwelt in swamplands farther to the south, but occasionally problems with the weather controllers would send packs of dragons north. The migration of dangerous species was a serious problem on the Frontier.

The motor home was already half-wrecked. Holes had been ripped in the roofs of both the cab and the living quarters, and the lesser dragons kept sticking their heads in. The situation was clear just from the smoking scraps of wood, the sleeping bags, and a pair of—partially eaten and barely recognizable human bodies lying in front of the motor home. Due to circumstances beyond their control—most likely something to do with their propulsion system—the family had been forced to camp out instead of sleeping in their vehicle like they should. But words couldn't begin to describe how foolhardy they'd been to expect one little campfire to keep the creatures that prowled the night at bay. There were three sleeping bags. But there weren't three corpses.

Once again a gunshot rang out, a streak of orange from a window in the living quarters split the darkness, and one of the dragons reeled back as the spot between its eyes exploded. For someone foolish enough to camp out at night, the shooter seemed well-informed and incredibly skilled with a gun. People who lived up north had usually never heard where to aim a kill-shot on southern creatures like these lesser dragons. But a solution to that puzzle soon presented itself. There was a large magneto-bike parked beside the vehicle. Someone was pitching in to rescue them.

The traveler tugged on the reins. Shaking off the moonlight that encrusted its body like so much dust, his cyborg horse suddenly began its descent. Galloping down the steep slope with the sort of speed normally reserved for level ground, the mount left a gale in its wake as it closed on the lesser dragons.

Noticing the headlong charge by this new foe, a dragon to the rear of the pack turned, and the horse and rider slipped by its side like a black wind. Bright blood didn't spout from between the creature's eyes until the horse had come to a sudden halt and the traveler had dismounted with a flourish of his cape. The way he walked toward the creatures—with their colossal maws gaping and rows of bloody teeth bared—seemed leisurely at first glance, but in due time showed the swiftness of a swallow in flight. All around the young man in black there was the sound of steel meeting steel time and time again. Unable to pull apart the jagged teeth they'd just brought together, each and every one of the lesser dragons around him collapsed in a bloody spray as gashes opened between their eyes. And the dragon leaping at him from the motor home's roof was no exception.

The young man's gorgeous countenance seemed weary of the cries of the dying creatures, but his expression didn't change in the slightest, and, without even glancing at the two mangled bodies, he returned his longsword to its sheath and headed back to his cyborg horse. As if to say he'd just done this on a lark, as if to suggest he didn't give a thought to the well-being of any survivors, he turned his back on this death-shrouded world and tightened his grip on the reins.

"Hey, wait a minute," a masculine voice called out in a somewhat agitated manner, and the young man finally stopped and turned around. The vehicle's door opened and a bearded man in a leather vest appeared. In his right hand he held a single-shot armor-piercing rifle. A machete was tucked through his belt. With the grim countenance he sported, he'd have looked more natural holding the latter instead of a gun. "Not that I don't appreciate your help, bucko, but there's no account for you just turning and making tracks like that now. Come here for a minute."

"There's only one survivor," the young man said. "And it's a child, so you should be able to handle it alone."

A tinge of surprise flooded the other man's hirsute face. "How did you . . . ? Ah, you saw the sleeping bags. Now wait just a minute, bucko. The atomic reactor has a cracked heat exchanger and the whole motor home's lousy with radiation now. That's why the family went outside in the first place. The kid got a pretty good dose."

"Hurry up and take care of it then."

"The supplies I'm packing won't cut it. A town doctor's gotta see to this. Where are you headed, buddy? The Zemeckis rendezvous point?"

"That's right," the young man in black replied.

"Hold on. Just hold everything. I know the roads around here like the back of my hand."

"So do I." The young man turned away from the biker once again. Then he stopped. As he turned back, his eyes were eternally cold and dark.

The child was standing behind the biker. Her black hair would've hung past her waist if it hadn't been tied back by a rainbow-hued ribbon. The rough cotton shirt and long skirt did little to hide her age, or the swell of her full bosom. The girl was a beauty, around seventeen or eighteen years old. As she gazed at the young man, a curious hue of emotion filled her eyes. There was something in the gorgeous features of the youth that could make her forget the heartrending loss of her family as well as the very real danger of losing her own life. Extending her hand, she was just about to say something when she crumpled to the ground face down.

"What did I tell you—she's hurt bad! She's not gonna last till dawn. That's why I need your help."

The youth wheeled his horse around without a word. "Which one of us will carry her?" he asked.

"Yours truly, of course. Getting you to help so far has been like pulling teeth, so I'll be damned if I'm gonna let you do the fun part."

The man got a leather belt off his bike and came back, then put the young woman on his back and cleverly secured her to himself. "Hands off," the man said, glaring at the youth in black as he straddled his magneto-bike. The girl fit perfectly into the seat behind him. It looked like quite a cozy arrangement. "Okay, here I go. Follow me." The man grabbed the handlebars, but, before twisting the grip starter, he turned and said, "That's right . . . I didn't introduce myself, did I? I'm John M. Brasselli Pluto VIII."

"D."

"That's a good name you got there. Just don't go looking to shorten mine for something a little easier to say. When you call me, I'll thank you kindly to do it by my full name. John M. Brasselli Pluto VIII, okay?" But, while the man was driving his point home, D was looking to the skies. "What is it?" the biker asked.

"Things out there have caught the scent of blood and are on their way."

The black creatures framed against the moon were growing closer. A flock of avian predators. And lupine howls could be heard in the wind.

†

Expectations to the contrary, no threat materialized to hamper the party's progress. They rode for about three hours. When the hazy mountains far across the plain began to fill their field of view and take on a touch of reality, John M. Brasselli Pluto VIII turned his sharp gaze to D, who rode alongside him. "If we go to the foot of that there mountain, the town should be by. What business you got with them anyway, bucko?" he asked, but when D made no answer he added, "Damn, playing the tough guy again, I see. I bet you're used to just standing there doing the strong, silent type routine and getting all the ladies, chum. You're good at what you do, I'll give you that—just don't count on that always doing the trick for you. Sooner or later, it's always some straight-shooter like me that ends up the center of attention."

D looked ahead without saying a word.

"Aw, you're no fun," the biker said. "I'm gonna gun it the rest of the way."

"Hold it."

Pluto VIII went pale for a minute at the sharp command, but, in what was probably a show of false courage, he soon gave the grip starter a good twist. Uranium fuel sent pale flames spouting from the boosters, and the bike shot off in a cloud of dust. It stopped almost as quickly. The engine was still shuddering away, but the wheels were just kicking up sand. In the dazzling moonlight, his atomic-powered bike was not only refusing to budge an inch despite its five thousand-horsepower output, it was actually sinking into the ground slowly but surely. "Dammit all," he hissed, "a sand viper!"

The creature in question was a colossal serpent that lived deep in the earth, and, although no one had ever seen the entire body of one, they were said to grow upwards of twenty miles long. Frighteningly enough, though the creatures were said to live their entire lives without ever moving a fraction of an inch, some believed they used high-frequency vibrations to create fragile layers of earth and sand in thousands of places on the surface so they might feed on those unfortunate enough to stumble into one of their traps. These layers moved relentlessly downward, becoming a kind of quicksand. Due to the startling motion the sands displayed, those who set foot into them would never make it out again. To get some idea of how tenacious the jaws of this dirt-and-sand trap were, one had only to watch how the five thousand horses in that atomic engine strained themselves to no avail. For all the bike's struggling, its wheels had already sunk halfway into the sand.

"Hey, don't just stand there watching, stone face. If you've got a drop of human blood in your veins, help me out here!" Pluto VIII shouted fervently. His words must've done the trick because D grabbed a thin coil of rope off the back of his saddle and dismounted. "If you screw this up, the rope'll get pulled down, too. So make your throw count," the man squawked, and then his eyes went wide. The gorgeous young man didn't throw him the rope. Keeping it in hand, he started to calmly walk into the quicksand. Pluto VIII opened his mouth to howl some new curse at the youth, but it just hung open . . . and for good reason.

The young man in black had started to stride elegantly over deadly jaws that would wolf down any creature they could find.

His black raiment danced in the wind, the moonlight ricocheting off it as flecks of silver. He almost looked like the Grim Reaper coming in the guise of aid, but ready to wrap a black cord around the neck of those reaching out to him for succor.

The rope flew through the air. Excitedly grabbing hold of the end of it, Pluto VIII tied it around his bike's handlebars. The rest of the coiled rope still in hand, D went back to solid ground and climbed onto his cyborg horse without saying a word.

"All right! Now on the count of—" Pluto never got to finish what he was saying as his bike was tugged forward. "Hey! Give me a second. Let me give it some gas, too," he started to say, but he only had a moment to tighten his grip on the throttle before the bike and its two riders were free of the living sands and its tires were resting once more on solid ground.

"Bucko, what the hell are you anyway?" Pluto VIII asked the mounted youth, with a shocked look on his face.. "We'd be lucky to get away from a sand viper with a tractor pulling us, never mind a cyborg horse. And here you go and yank us out without even working up a sweat . . . I thought you was a mite too good-looking, but you're not human after all, are you?" Smacking his hands together, he exclaimed, "I've got it—you're a dhampir!"

D didn't move. His eternally cold gaze was fixed on the moonlit reaches of the darkness, as if seeking a safe path.

"But you don't have anything to worry about," the biker added. "My motto is 'Keep an open mind.' It don't matter if the folks around me have red skin or green—I don't discriminate. So long as they don't do wrong by yours truly, that is. Naturally, that includes dhampirs, too." Pluto VIII's voice had the ring of unquestionable sincerity to it.

Suddenly, without even glancing at the biker who seemed ready to burst with the milk of human kindness, D asked in a low voice, "Are you ready?"

"For what?" Pluto VIII must've caught something in the Hunter's disinterested tone, because his eyes went to D, then instantly swept around to the left and right, to the fore and rear. Aside from the piece of land the three of them were on, little black holes were forming all over the place. As sand coursed down into them the way it does into an antlion pit, the funnel-shaped holes quickly grew larger until one touched another, encircling the trio like the footprints of some unseen giant.

II

S on of a bitch . . . Don't seem like this freakin' sand viper aims to let us out of here alive," Pluto VIII said, the laughter strong in his voice. Sometimes a bit of cheer came to him in the midst of utter despair, but that had nothing to do with Pluto VIII's laugh, still full of confidence and hope.

But how on earth could they get themselves out of this mess? It didn't look like even D, with all his awesome skill, could get out of these preposterously large antlion pits. Especially since he wasn't alone. His traveling companion had a young woman strapped to his back, and, since she was suffering from extreme radiation poisoning, time was of the essence.

"Hey, what do we do?" Pluto VIII asked, looking extremely interested in the answer.

"Close your eyes and duck!" came the harsh reply.

Pluto VIII didn't have the faintest idea what was going on, but the instant he complied the whole world filled with white light. Under the pillar of light stretching down to the bottom of the colossal funnel, grains of sand grew super-hot, bubbled, and cooled almost instantly into a glassy plain reflecting the moon. The pillar of light silently stretched to the sky time and again, and, as D squinted ever so slightly at this mixing of light and darkness, his face was at times starkly lit, at other times deep in shadow. It seemed to go on for ages, but it couldn't have taken more than a few seconds. Aside from the dim, white depressions gleaming like water, the moonlit plain was just as it'd been before—deathly still.

"Looks like an atomic blast blew the hell out of the sand viper holes—melted 'em and turned 'em to glass. Who the hell could've done that?" Pluto VIII asked, and then he once again followed D's gaze. He might've been well-informed, but a gasp of wonder escaped from him nonetheless.

A black shadow that seemed both circular and oblong clung to the central part of the distant mountain range. It wasn't on the mountain's rocky walls. The shadowy shape was crossing the mountain peaks. Not only that, but, as it slowly moved forward, it was clearly coming lower as well. Taking the distance into consideration, it must've been moving at a speed of twelve or thirteen miles per hour at least. It was round, and about two miles in diameter.

"So, we have them to thank then?" Pluto VIII asked.

D gave a negligible nod. "Good thing there's still a mobile town around equipped with a Prometheus cannon. Incredible marksmanship, too. Our saviors got here right on schedule."

"Well, thank heaven for that. I just hope the mayor ain't the kind of guy who'll expect us to return the favor. Let's go," said the biker, "I don't feel like waiting around for the town to get here!"

The bike's boosters roared and the thud of iron-shod hoofs on earth echoed across the plain. After they'd run at full speed for a good ten minutes, the huge black shape floated up over the crest of a hill before them like a cloud. The bottom was covered with spheres constructed of iron and wood, as well as with pipes. The white smoke erupting from the latter indicated that compressed air was one of the types of energy driving the cloud forward. And yet, how much thrust would be necessary just to move this thing an inch? After all, this massive structure that made the earth tremble as it came over the slope and slowly slid down it was a whole town. Even knowing that, even seeing it up close, it was no easy task to comprehend something so awesome. The town must've covered more than two square miles. On top of a massive circular base some thirty feet high, buildings of wood, plastic, and iron were clustered together. Between them ran streets, some straight and orderly, others twisting and capricious. At the edge of the densely packed buildings there was a small park and a cluster of tombstones that marked the cemetery. Of course, in addition to the residential sector, the structure boasted everything found in an ordinary village or town—a hospital, a sheriff's office, a jail, and a fire station. In the park, live trees swayed with the wind.

Startlingly enough, the base that supported this colossal establishment and was indispensable in its smooth movement hovered some three feet off the ground. That wasn't something just compressed-air jets or rocket engines could manage. No doubt power produced by the atomic reactor inside the base was run through a subatomic particle-converter and changed to antigravity energy. Still, to keep the structure a good three feet off the ground, there had to be some secret to the output of their atomic reactor or the capacity of their converters.

The base loomed blackly before the two men, and the mechanical whoosh blew closer and closer. A blinding light flashed down on the trio of travelers from a platform near the iron inlay on the top edge of the base. A question boomed over the speakers. "What do you folks want?"

Pluto VIII pulled the mic from his bike to his mouth and answered, "We're travelers. And we got an injured person here. We'd like to have a doctor take a look at 'er. Would you let us in?"

There was silence. The searchlight continued to shine on the trio. Well-concealed guns no doubt had them locked in their crosshairs. After a while, there was a reply. "No can do. We're not taking on any new blood. The town's population is already thirty percent over what our resources can support. Find yourselves another town or village. The closest one's twelve and a half miles from here—a place by the name of Hahiko."

"You've gotta be yanking my chain!" Pluto VIII growled, pounding a fist against his handlebars. "Who the hell's talking about twelve and a half miles?! Look, this girl I've got on my back's been doused real bad with radiation. She couldn't make it another hundred yards, let alone twelve and a half miles. What are you, the freaking Nobility?!"

"Nothing you can say's gonna make any difference," the voice said coldly. "These orders come from the mayor. On top of that, the girl is part of the Knight family—Lori's her name. Two and a half months back they left town, so we're not about to let one of them back in now."

"I don't give a rat's ass about that. We got a girl in the prime of her life about to die. What, don't any of you have kids?"

The voice fell silent again. When another announcement rang out, it was a different person's voice. "We're set to roll," the new speaker said, "so clear the way!" And then, sounding somewhat agitated, he added, "Hey, young fellah—you wouldn't happen to be named D, would you?"

The youth nodded slightly.

"Oh, you should've said so in the first place. I'm the one who sent for you. Mayor Ming's the name. Just a second and we'll let you on board."

Machinery groaned, the iron door rose upward, and a boarding ramp started to glide out.

D said softly, "I've got some companions."

"Companions?!" Mayor Ming's voice quavered. "I'd always heard you were the most aloof, independent Hunter on earth. Just when did you get these companions?"

"Earlier."

"Earlier? You mean those two?"

"Do you see anyone else?" the Hunter asked.

"No—it's just . . . "

"I've fought side by side with them. That's the only reason I have. But if you have no business with me, I'll be on my way."

"W . . . wait a minute." The mayor's tone shifted from vacillating to determined. "We can't afford to lose you. I'll make a special exception for them. Come aboard."

The earth shook as the broad boarding-ramp hit the ground. Once the travelers were on, along with the bike and the cyborg horse, the ramp began to rise once again.

"The nerve of these people and their overblown escalator," Pluto VIII carped unabashedly.

As soon as the ramp had retracted into the town's base, an iron door shut behind them and the two men found themselves in a vast chamber that reeked of oil. A number of armed men in the prime of life and a gray-haired old man stood there. The latter was more muscular in build than the men who surrounded him. Mayor Ming, no doubt. He may have had trouble walking, as he carried a steel cane in his right hand. "Glad you could make it," he said. "I'm Ming."

"Introductions can wait," Pluto VIII bellowed. "Where's the doctor?"

The mayor gave a nod, and two men stepped forward and unstrapped the girl—Lori—from the biker's back. "I imagine your companion's more interested in eating than hearing us talk business," the mayor said, signaling the other men with his eyes.

"Damn straight—you read my mind. Well, I'm off then, D. See you later."

When Pluto had disappeared through a side door following his guides at his own leisurely pace, the mayor led D to a passageway that continued up to the next level. The whistling of the wind seemed to know no end. All around them, ash-colored scenery rolled by. Forests and mountains. The town was moving across Innocent Prairie, the second of the Frontier's great plains. Whipping the Hunter's pitch black cape and tossing his long, black hair, the wind blurred the wilds around them like a distant watercolor scene.

"How do you like the view?" Mayor Ming made a wave of one arm as if mowing down the far reaches of the plain. "Majestic, isn't it?" he said. Perhaps he'd taken the lack of expression on the young man staring off into the darkness as an expression of wonder. "The town maintains a cruising speed of twelve miles per hour.

She can climb any mountain range or cliff, so long as it's less than a sixty-degree incline. Of course, we can only do that when we give the engines a blanket infusion of antigravity energy. This is how we always guarantee our five hundred residents a safe and comfortable journey."

"A comfortable journey, you say?" D muttered, but his words might not have reached the mayor's ears. "That's fine, as long as wherever you're headed is safe and comfortable, too. What do you want with me?"

The Hunter's hair flew in the wind that howled across the darkened sky. They were standing on an observation platform set at the very front of the town. If this had been a ship, it would've been the bow—or perhaps the prow. Jutting as it did from the top of the town's base, it seemed like it'd be the perfect spot to experience wind and rain and all the varied aspects of the changing seasons.

"Don't you care how that girl Lori's doing?" the mayor asked, ignoring D's inquiry.

"Stick to business."

"Hmm. A man who can slice a laser beam in two, who's discarded all human emotion . . . You're just like the stories make you out to be. I don't care how thick the Noble blood runs in you dhampirs, you could stand to act a tad more human."

D turned to leave without making a sound.

"Come now. Don't go yet. Aren't you the hasty one," the mayor called, not seeming particularly overanxious. "There's only one reason anyone ever calls a Vampire Hunter—and that's for killing Nobility."

D turned back.

"When I let that man on two hundred years ago, I never in my wildest dreams would've thought something like this could happen," the mayor muttered. "That was the biggest mistake of my life."

D brushed his billowing hair back with his left hand.

"He was standing at the foot of the Great Northern Mountains, all alone. When we had him in the spotlight, he looked like the very darkness condensed. Now as a rule this town doesn't take on folks we just meet along the way, but it might've been the way he looked that stopped us dead in our tracks. There was a deep, dark look to his eyes. Come to think of it, he looked a lot like you."

The wind filled the sudden gap in conversation. After a pause, the mayor continued. "As soon as he was aboard, he came up here to the deck and looked out at the nocturnal wilds and rugged chain of mountains for the longest time. And then he calmly turned to me and said, 'Choose from the townsfolk five men and five women of surpassing strength and intellect, that they may join me in my travels.' Of course, I had to chuckle at that. At which point he laughed like thunder and said, 'Agree to my offer, and your people will know a thousand years of glory. Refuse, and this town will be cursed for all eternity to wander the deadly wilds,'" said the mayor, breaking off there. Pitch-black fatigue clung to his powerful and strangely smooth face. "Then he was gone. A touch of anxiety filled my heart, but nothing happened to the town after that. The next two hundred years weren't exactly one continuous stretch of peace and prosperity, but now I think I can safely say they were times of pure bliss. Now the dark days are upon us. If this town is indeed under a curse as he decreed, we shall never be graced with glory or prosperity again."

Perhaps the reason the mayor had invited the Vampire Hunter up onto the deck was to show him the deadly wilds of their destiny.

"Come with me," Mayor Ming said. "I'll show you the real problem at hand."

†

A girl lay on a simple bed. Even without seeing her paraffin-pale skin or the wounds at the base of her throat, it was clear she was a victim of the Nobility. The most unsettling thing about her was her eyes—she had them trained on the ceiling, but they still had the spark of life.

"This is my daughter Laura. She's almost eighteen," said the mayor.

D didn't move, but remained looking down at the pale throat against the pillow.

"Three weeks ago she started acting strangely," said Mayor Ming. "I picked up on it when she said she thought she was coming down with a cold and started wearing a scarf. I never would've dreamed it could happen. It's just impossible we'd have a Noble in our town of all places."

"Has she been bitten again since then?"

At D's icy words, the distraught mayor nodded his head. "Twice. Both at night. We had one of our fighting men watching over her each time, but both times they were asleep before they knew it. Laura keeps losing more and more blood, but we've seen hide nor hair of the Nobility."

"You've done checks, haven't you?"

"Five times—and thorough ones at that. Everyone in town can walk in the light of day."

But D knew that such a test wasn't proof-positive that one of the townspeople wasn't a vampire. "We'll run another check later," D said, "but tonight I'll stay with her."

A shade of relief found its way into the mayor's steely expression. Though the man had lived more than two centuries, apparently at heart he was just like any other father. "I'd appreciate that. Can I get you anything?"

"I'm fine," D replied.

"If I may be so bold, could I say something?" The firm tone reminded the mayor and Hunter there was someone else present. A young physician stood by the door with his arms folded. Making no effort to conceal the anger in his face, he glared at D.

"Pardon me, Dr. Tsurugi. You have some objection to all this?" the mayor said, bowing to the young man who'd interrupted them.

The doctor had been introduced to D when the mayor brought the Hunter to his daughter's room. He was a young circuit doctor who traveled from village to village out on the Frontier. Like D, he had black hair and dark eyes, and there didn't appear to be much difference in their ages. But, of course, as a dhampir D's age wasn't exactly clear, so external appearances were useless for comparisons.

The young physician shook his intelligent yet still somewhat innocent face from side to side. "No, I have no objection. Since there's nothing more I can do for her as a physician, I'll entrust the next step to this Hunter. However—"

"Yes?" said the mayor.

"I would like to keep watch over Ms. Laura with him. I realize I might sound out of line here, but I believe it's part of my duty as her physician."

Mayor Ming pensively tapped the handle of his cane against his forehead. While he probably considered the young physician's request perfectly natural, he also must've wished Dr. Tsurugi had never suggested such a troubling arrangement.

Before the mayor could turn to the Hunter, D replied, "If my opponent can't escape, there'll be a fight. I won't be able to keep you out of harm's way."

"I can look out for myself."

"Even if it means you might get bitten by one of them?" asked the Hunter.

Anyone who lived on the Frontier understood the implication of those words, and for a heartbeat the hot-blooded doctor's expression stiffened with fear, but then he replied firmly, "That's a chance I'm willing to take." His eyes seemed to blaze with intensity as he gazed at D. It might've been fair to say he was glaring at the Hunter.

Without giving his reply so much as a nod, D said, "Not a chance."

"But, why the—I mean, why not? I said quite clearly I was prepared to—"

"If by some chance something were to happen to you, it would turn the whole town against me."

"But that's just . . . " Dr. Tsurugi started to say. His face was flush with crimson anger, but he bit his lip and choked back any further contentions.

"Well, then, I'd like you both to step outside now. I have some questions for the girl," D said coolly, looking to the door. That was the signal for them to leave. There was something about the young man that could destroy any will to resist they still had.

As the mayor and Dr. Tsurugi turned to leave, the wooden door in front of them creaked open.

"Hey, how are you doing, tough guy?" someone said in a cheery voice. The face that poked into the room belonged to none other than John M. Brasselli Pluto VIII.

"How did you get here?" the mayor asked sharply.

"I, er . . . I'm terribly sorry, sir," said one of the townsfolk behind the biker—apparently a guard. "You wouldn't believe how stubborn this guy is, and he's strong as an ox."

"Don't have a fit now, old-timer," Pluto VIII said, smiling amiably. "I figured D'd probably be at your place. And it's not like there's anyone in town who doesn't know where the mayor lives. Anyhow—D, I found out how the girl's doing. That's what I came to tell you."

"I already told him some time ago," Dr. Tsurugi said with disdain. "He learned about her condition while you were busy eating."

"What the hell?! Am I the last one to know or something?!" Pluto VIII scratched wildly at a beard that looked as dense as the jungle does when seen from the air. "Okay, no big deal. C'mon, D! Let's go pay her a visit."

"You do it."

As the gorgeous young man leaned over the bed just as indifferent as he was before, Pluto asked him, "What gives, bucko? You risk your life saving a young lady and then you don't even wanna see if she's getting better? What, is the mayor's daughter so all-fired important?"

"This is business."

Pluto VIII had no way of knowing that it was nothing short of a miracle for D to answer such a contentious question. With an indignant look on his face matching that of the nearby physician, the biker pushed his way through the doorway. "Damn, I don't believe your nerve," he cursed. Spittle flew from his lips. "Do you *really* know how she's doing? She's got level-three radiation poisoning to her speech center, and just as much damage to her sense of hearing to boot. And neither of them can be fixed. She's got some slight burns on her skin, too, but supplies of artificial skin are limited and since it's not life threatening they'll leave her the way she is. How's that strike you? She's at the tender age where girls look up at the stars and weep, and now she's gonna have to carry the memory of watching her folks get eaten alive, her body is dotted with burns, and to top everything off she can't freakin' talk or hear no more."

More than the tragic details of what was essentially the utter ruin of that young woman, it was Pluto's righteous indignation that made the mayor and Dr. Tsurugi lower their eyes.

D quietly replied, "I listened to what you had to say. Now get out."

III

Once the clamorous Pluto VIII had been pulled away from the room by the mayor and four guards, D looked down at Laura's face. Vacant as her gaze was, her eyes were still invested with a strange vitality, and they suddenly came into focus. The cohesive will she'd kept hidden tinged her eyes red. The will of a Noble. A breath howled out of her mouth. Like the corrupting winds gusting through the gates of Hell.

"What did you come here for?" she asked. Her eyes practically dripped venom as they stabbed back at D's. Laura's lips warped.

Something could be seen glistening between her lips and overly active tongue. Canine teeth. Once again Laura said, "What are you here for?"

"Who defiled you?" asked D.

"Defiled me?" The girl's lips twisted into a grin. "To keep feeling the pleasure I've known, I wish I could be defiled night and day. What are you? I know you're not just an ordinary traveler. We don't get many folks around here who use words like defile."

"What time will he be here?"

"Well, now . . . Suppose you ask him yourself?" Her pleased expression suddenly stiffened. All the evil and rapture was stripped away like a thin veneer, and for a brief moment an innocent expression befitting a slumbering girl of eighteen skimmed across her face. Then, once again her features became as expressionless as paraffin. Dawn had come at last to the Great Northern Plains.

D raised his left hand and placed it on the young woman's forehead. "Exactly who or what attacked you?"

Consciousness returned to her cadaverous face. "I don't . . . know. Eyes, two red eyes . . . getting closer . . . but it's . . . "

"Is it someone from town?" asked D.

"I don't know . . . "

"When were you attacked?"

"Three weeks ago . . . in the park . . . " Laura answered slowly. "It was pitch black . . . Just those burning eyes . . . "

"When will he come next?"

"Oh . . . tonight . . . tonight . . . " Laura's body snapped tight, like a giant steel spring had suddenly formed inside her. The blankets flew off her with the force of it. She let out what sounded like a death rattle, the tongue lolled out of her mouth, and then her body began to rise in the most fascinating way. This paranormal phenomenon often occurred when a victim's dependency to the Nobility was pitted against some power bent on destroying that bond. Hunters frequently had an opportunity to observe this behavior, so D's expression didn't change a whit. But then, this young man's expression probably wouldn't show shock in a million years.

"Looks like that's all we'll be getting," said a hoarse voice that came from between the young woman's brow and the hand that rested against it. "The girl doesn't know anything aside from what she's told us. Guess we'll have to ask her little friend after all."

When the Hunter's hand was removed, Laura crashed back down onto the bed. Waiting until light as blue as water speared in through the window, D left the room. The mayor was waiting for him outside.

"Learned something in there, did you?" said Mayor Ming. He demonstrated the mentality of those who lived out on the Frontier by not asking the Hunter if he could save her or not.

The fact of the matter was, when a vampire with a victim in the works learned that a Hunter had come for him or her, they'd make themselves scarce unless the victim was especially dear to them. After that, it was all just a matter of time. The future of that victim might vary depending on how many times he or she'd been bitten, and how much blood had been taken. There were some who could go on to live a normal life even after five fateful visits to their bedroom—though they usually became social outcasts. But there were also some young ladies whose skin turned to pale paraffin from a single cursed kiss, and they'd lie in bed forever waiting for their caller to come again, never aging another day. And then one day a victim's gray-haired grandchildren and great-grandchildren would suddenly see her limbs shrivel like an old mummy's and know that somewhere out in the wide world the accursed Noble had finally met its fate. The question was, just how long would that take? How many living dead were still out there, sustained by nothing but moonlight, hiding in the corner of some rotting, dusty ruins, their kith and kin all long since dead? Time wasn't on the side of those who walked in the light of day.

"Tonight, we'll be having a visitor," D told the mayor.

"Oh, well that's just—"

"Is your daughter the only victim?"

The mayor nodded. "So far. But as long as whoever did this is still out there, that number could swell until it includes every one of us."

"I'd like you to prepare something for me," D said as he looked to the blue sky beyond the window.

"Just name it. If it's a room you need, we've already prepared your accommodations."

"No, I'd like a map of your town and data on all the residents," said D. "Also, I need to know everywhere the town has gone since it started its journey, and what destinations are set for the future."

"Understood," said the mayor.

"Where will my quarters be?"

"I'll show you the way."

"No need to do that," the Hunter replied.

"It's a single family house near the park. A bit old, perhaps, but it's made of wood. It's located . . . " After the mayor finished relating the directions, he pushed down on the grip of his cane with both hands and muttered, "It'd be nice if we could get this all settled tonight."

"Where was your daughter attacked?" D asked.

"In a vacant house over by the park. Didn't find anything there when we checked it out, though. It's not far from the house we have for you, either."

D asked for the location, and the mayor gave it to him.

Then D went outside. The wind had died down. Only its whistling remained. There must've been a device somewhere in town for projecting a shield over the entire structure. The town's defenses against the harsh forces of nature were indeed perfect. Blue light made the Hunter stand out starkly as he went down the street. The shadow he cast on the ground was faint. That was a dhampir's lot. There was no sign of the living in the residential sector. For the tranquil hours of night, people became like breathing corpses.

Up ahead, the Hunter could see a tiny point of light. A bit of warmth beckoning to the dawn's first light. A hospital. D walked past it without saying a word. He didn't seem to be looking at the signs that marked each street. His pace was like the wind.

After about twenty minutes he was out of the residential section, and he stopped just as the trees of the park came into view. To his right was a row of half-cylindrical buildings—one of them was his destination. That's where young Laura had been attacked. The mayor had told him all of the buildings were vacant. At first, that'd only been true for the building in question, but, after the incident involving Laura, the families living nearby had requested other quarters and moved out. Dilapidation was already creeping up on the structures.

The house on the end was the only one shut tight by poles and locks. The fact that it'd been sealed with heavy poles instead of ordinary planks made it clear how panicked the people were. And there were five locks on the door—all electronic.

D reached for the locks. The pendant at his breast gave off a blue light, and, at the mere touch of his pale fingertips, the locks dropped to his feet. Soon his fingers closed on the poles, which had been fixed in a gigantic X. The poles of unmilled wood were over eight inches in diameter and had been riveted in place. D's hand wouldn't wrap even halfway around one. It didn't look like there'd be any way for him to get a good grip on them. But his fingertips sank into the bark. His left hand tore both poles free with one tug.

Pushing his way past a door that'd lost its paint in the same crisscrossing shape, D headed inside. A stench pervaded the place. It was the kind of stink that called to mind colors—colors beyond counting. And each of them painted its own repulsive image. As if something ominous beyond telling was drifting through the dilapidated house.

Though the windows were all boarded up, D casually advanced down the dark hallway, coming to the room where they'd found Laura. As the mayor had said, they'd performed an exhaustive search, and anything that wasn't nailed down had been taken out of the room. There were no tables, chairs, or doors here. D's unconcerned eyes moved ever so slightly as he stood in the center of the room.

He stepped out into the hall without making a sound. At the end of another hall that ran perpendicular to the first he could see the door to the next room. A shadow tumbled through the doorway. It was like a stain of indeterminate shape. Its contours shifted like seaweed underwater, and the center of it eddied. Then it stood up. A pair of legs were visible. A head and torso were vaguely discernible. It was a human wrapped in some kind of protective membrane. What on earth was it doing here?

D advanced slowly.

The stain didn't move. Its hands and feet changed shape from one moment to the next, yet their respective functions remained clear.

"What are you?" D asked softly. Though his tone was quiet, it had a ring to it that made it clear his questions weren't to be left unanswered, much less ignored. "What are you doing here? Answer me."

Swaying all the while, the stain charged at him. It was a narrow hallway. D had no way of avoiding it. His right hand went for the longsword on his back—and dead ahead of him, his foe waved its arm. A black disk zipped off toward D's face.

Narrowly ducking his head, D drew his longsword. Seeming to have some special insight into the situation, the Hunter didn't use his unsheathed weapon to parry the disk, but slashed with the blade from ground to sky. His foe had already halted its charge, and now a terrific white light flashed through its crotch. From the bottom up, his foe was bisected. And yet, aside from a slight ripple that ran through its whole body, the shifting shadow was unchanged. An indescribable sound echoed behind it. Regardless, D advanced.

Without making a sound, the shadow backed against the wall behind it. It certainly seemed just like a real shadow, because its clearly three-dimensional form abruptly lost its depth and became perfectly flat before being completely and silently absorbed by the wall. D stood before the wall without saying a word. The gray surface of the tensile plastic was glowing faintly. That was the aftereffect of molecular intangibility—the ability to pass through walls without resistance. The process of altering cellular atomic-structure and passing through the molecules of some barrier caused subtle changes in radioactive isotopes. That same ability had probably allowed the shadow to evade the blow from D's sword.

Doing an about-face, D ran his eyes across either side of the hallway. The disk had vanished. There were no signs it'd hit anything, either.

D pushed open the same door the shadow had come from. It appeared to be a laboratory that'd been sealed in faint darkness. The walls were covered with all sorts of medicines, and the lab table bolted to the floor was covered with burn marks and was heavily discolored by stains. He noticed signs that some sort of mechanical device had been removed.

D came to a halt in the center of the room. There were shields over the windows. What kind of experiments had been performed here in the darkness, sealed away from the light? There was something extremely tragic about the place.

This was where the intruder had come from. Had it been living in here? Or had it slipped in before D arrived, searching for something? Probably the latter. In which case, it would be relatively easy to discover who it was. Five hundred people lived in this town. Finding the intruder among that many people wouldn't be impossible.

206 | H I D E Y U K I K I K U C H I

D went outside. There was something in this house. But he couldn't put his finger on what exactly it was. The sunlight gracing the world grew whiter. D came to a halt at the door. A black cloud was moving down the street. A mass of people. A mob. It almost looked like every person in town was there. The intense hostility and fear in their eyes made it quite plain they were fully aware of D's true nature.

D calmly made his way to the street. A black wall of a man suddenly loomed before him. He must've been about six foot eight and weighed around three hundred and thirty pounds. The giant had pectorals so wide and thick they looked like scales off a greater fire dragon. Leaving about three feet between them, D looked up at the man.

"Hey—you're a dhampir, ain't you?" The giant's deep voice was soaked with vermilion menace.

D didn't answer him.

Something flowed across the man's features like water. A frightened hue. He'd looked into D's eyes. It was another ten seconds or so before he managed to squeeze out another word. "Seeing where the mayor called you to his house, there ain't much we can do about you. But this here's a town for clean-living folk. We don't want no Noble half-breed hanging around, okay?"

The heads of those around him moved in unison. Nodding their agreement. There were men and women there, and even children.

"There's Nobility here. Or someone who serves them," D said softly. "The next family attacked might be yours."

"If it comes to that, we'll take care of it ourselves," said the giant. "We don't need no help from the Nobility's side."

Nodding faintly, D took a step. That alone was enough to part the fearful crowd. The giant and the others moved back like the outgoing tide.

"Wait just a damn minute!" Embarrassed perhaps to be afraid, the giant unleashed a tone that had a fierceness born of hysteria to it. "I'm gonna pound the shit out of you now, buster."

While he said this, the giant slipped on a pair of black leather gloves. The backs of them looked like plain leather, but the palms were covered with thin, flexible metal fibers. When the giant smacked his hands together, it set off clusters of purple sparks that stretched out like coral branches. People backed away speechless. Electromagnetic gloves like these were used by huntsmen. The highest setting on them was fifty thousand volts. Capable of killing a mid-sized fire dragon, they were lethal weapons to be sure.

"What are you, scumbag—half human? Or is it a third?" the giant sneered. "Whatever the hell it is, you're just lucky you're sort of like us. Now say your prayers that the only part of you I burn to a crisp is your filthy Noble blood." Purple sparks dyed his rampaging self-confidence a grotesque hue.

D started to walk away, completely oblivious. The giant ran at him, right hand raised and ready for action. D's movements and his expression were unchanged. Like shadows that'd never known the light.

A sharp glint of light burned through the air. The giant shook his hand in pain. Sparks leapt wildly from his palm, and then a slim scalpel fell to the ground.

"What the hell are you doing?!" The giant's enraged outburst went past D and straight on down the street. Coming toward them with determined strides, his lab coat crisp and white, was none other than Dr. Tsurugi. "Oh, it's you, Doc," the big man said. "What the hell are you trying to do?" Though he tried his best to sound threatening, there was no doubt the giant had the recognizable threat of the physician's scalpel-throwing to thank for the slight tremble to his voice.

Coming to a stop in front of thecrowd, Dr. Tsurugi said sharply, "Would you knock it off? This man is a guest of the mayor. Instead of trying to chase him off, you should be working with him to find the Nobility. Mr. Berg!" An elderly man, older than anyone one else there, seemed shaken by the physician's call. "You were right here—why didn't you put a stop to this? If we lose our Hunter, it stands to reason the Nobility will remain at large. As you'll recall, all *our* searches have ended in failure."

"I, er . . . yeah, I thought so, too. It's just . . . " Berg stammered ashamedly, "well, if he was a regular Hunter it'd be one thing. But him being a dhampir and all, I knew they wouldn't go for it. You know, the women and children been scared stiff since they heard the rumors he was here."

"And they can get by with just a good scare—a Noble will do far worse to them, I assure you," Dr. Tsurugi said grimly.

"B . . . but, Doc," a middle-aged woman cradling a baby stammered, "they say dhampirs do it, too. I hear when they're thirsty, they drink the blood of people they're working for . . . "

"Damned if that ain't the truth," the giant bellowed. "See, it ain't like we got no grounds for complaining. The whole damn town may be on the move, but information still gets in. Y'all remember what happened in Peamond, right?"

That was the name of a village where half the townsfolk had died of blood loss in a single night. Descending from the Nobility, dhampirs had a will of iron, but on occasion their spirit could succumb to the sweet siren call of blood. The man who'd been hired in Peamond found the black bonds of blood he'd tried so long to keep in check stirred anew by the beauty of the mayor's daughter, and then the Hunter himself became one of those he hunted. Before the inhabitants of the village got together and held him down long enough to drive a stake through his heart, the toll of victims had reached twenty-four.

"That's the grandfather of all exceptions." There was no vacillation whatsoever in Dr. Tsurugi's tone. "I happen to have the latest statistics. The proportion of dhampirs who've caused that sort of tragedy while on the job is no more than one twenty thousandth of a percent."

"And what proof do we have that this ain't gonna be one of those cases?!" the giant shouted. "We sure as hell don't wanna wind up that fucking one twenty thousandth of a percent. Ain't that right, folks?"

A number of voices rose in agreement.

"Come to think of it, Doc, you ain't from around here, neither. What's the story? You covering for him because you outsiders gotta stick together or something? I bet that's it—the two of you dirty dogs been in cahoots all along, ain't you?!"

All expression faded from Dr. Tsurugi's face. He stepped forward, saying, "You wanna do this with those gloves on? Or are you gonna take them off?"

The giant face twisted. And formed a smile. "Oh, this'll be good," he said, switching off the gloves and pulling them from his hands. From the expression on his face, you'd think he was the luckiest man on earth. The way the physician had nailed him with a scalpel earlier was pretty impressive, but aside from that he was only about five foot eight and tipped the scales at around a hundred and thirty-five pounds. The giant had strangled a bear before, so, when it came down to bare-knuckle brawling, he was supremely confident in his powerful arms.

"You sure you wanna do that, Conroy?" Berg asked, hustling in front of the giant to stop him. "What do you reckon they'll do to you if you bust up our doctor? You won't get no slap on the wrist, that's for damn sure!"

"So what—they'll give me a few lashes and shock me a couple of times? Hell, I'm used to it. Tell you what—I'll leave the doc's head and hands in one piece when I bust him up." Roughly shoving Berg out of the way, the giant stepped forward.

As the young physician also took a step forward, D called out from behind him, "Why don't you call it quits? This started out as my fight, after all."

"Well, it's mine now, so I'll thank you to just stand back and watch."

The air whistled. It could've been Conroy letting out his breath, or the whine of his punch ripping through the wind. Dr.

210 | HIDEYUKI KIKUCHI

Tsurugi jumped to the side to dodge a right hook as big and hard as a rock. As if the breeze from the punch had whisked him away. The young physician had both hands up in front of his chest in lightly clenched fists. How many of the people there noticed the calluses covering his knuckles, though? Narrowly avoiding the uppercut the giant threw as his second punch, Dr. Tsurugi let his left hand race into action. The path it traveled was a straight line.

To Conroy, it looked like everything past the physician's wrist had vanished. He felt three quick impacts on his solar plexus. The first two punches he took in stride, but the third one did the trick. He tried to exhale, but his wind caught in his throat. The physician's blows had a power behind them one would never imagine from his unassuming frame.

A bolt of beige lightning shot out at the giant's wobbling legs. No one there had ever seen such footwork. The physician's leg limned an elegant arc that struck the back of Conroy's knee, and the giant flopped to the ground with an earthshaking thud. Straight, thrusting punches from the waist and circular kicks— there'd been no hesitation in the chain of mysterious attacks, and how powerful they were soon became apparent as Conroy quickly started to get back up. As soon as the giant tried to put any weight on his left knee, he howled in pain and fell on his side.

"Probably won't be able to stand for the rest of the day," the young physician said, looking around at the chalk-white faces of the people as if nothing had happened. "Just goes to show it doesn't pay to go around whipping up mobs. All of you move along now. Back to your homes."

"Yeah, but, Doc," a man with a long, gourd-shaped face said as he pointed to Conroy, "who's gonna see to his wounds?"

"I'll have a look at him," Dr. Tsurugi said with resignation. "Bring him by the hospital some time. Just don't do it for about three days or so. Looks like it'll take him that long to cool down. But from here on out, there's a damn good chance I'll refuse to treat anyone who raises a hand to the Hunter here, so keep that in mind. Okay, move along now." After he'd seen to it that the people dispersed and Conroy had been carried away, Dr. Tsurugi turned to face D.

"That's a remarkable skill you have," the Hunter said. "I recall seeing it in the East a long time ago. What is it?"

"It's called karate. My grandfather taught it to me. But I'm surprised you'd put up with so much provocation."

"I didn't have to. You put an end to it. Maybe you did it to keep me from having to hurt any of the locals . . . Whatever the reason, you helped me out."

"No, I didn't." There was mysterious light in the physician's eyes as he shook his head. While you couldn't really call it amity, it wasn't hostility or enmity, either. You might call it a kind of tenacity.

And then D asked him, "Have we met somewhere before?"

"No, never," the physician said, shaking his head. "As I told you, I'm a circuit doctor. In my rounds out on the Frontier, I've heard quite a few stories about you."

The physician looked like he had more to say, but D interrupted him, asking, "Who used to live in that abandoned house?"

The physician's eyes went wide. "You mean to tell me you didn't know before you went in? The house belongs to Lori Knight—the girl you rescued."

To be continued in

VAMPIRE HUNTER D

VOLUME 4
TALE OF THE DEAD TOWN

now available at your favorite bookseller

ABOUT THE AUTHOR

Hideyuki Kikuchi was born in Chiba, Japan in 1949. He attended the prestigious Aoyama University and wrote his first novel *Demon City Shinjuku* in 1982. Over the past two decades, Kikuchi has authored numerous horror novels, and is one of Japan's leading horror masters, writing novels in the tradition of occidental horror authors like Fritz Leiber, Robert Bloch, H. P. Lovecraft, and Stephen King. As of 2004, there were seventeen novels in his hugely popular ongoing Vampire Hunter D series. Many live action and anime movies of the 1980s and 1990s have been based on Kikuchi's novels.

ABOUT THE ILLUSTRATOR

Yoshitaka Amano was born in Shizuoka, Japan. He is well known as a manga and anime artist and is the famed designer for the Final Fantasy game series. Amano took part in designing characters for many of Tatsunoko Productions' greatest cartoons, including *Gatchaman* (released in the U.S. as *G-Force* and *Battle of the Planets*). Amano became a freelancer at the age of thirty and has collaborated with numerous writers, creating nearly twenty illustrated books that have sold millions of copies. Since the late 1990s Amano has worked with several American comics publishers, including DC Comics on the illustrated Sandman novel *Sandman: The Dream Hunters* with Neil Gaiman and *Elektra and Wolverine: The Redeemer* with best-selling author Greg Rucka.